UNTIL
DEATH
DO US
PART

BONZAI
MOON

BonzaiMoon Books LLC
Houston, Texas
www.bonzaimoonbooks.com

This is a work of fiction. Names, characters, places and incidents either are the product of the authors' imaginations or are used fictitiously, and any resemblance to actual persons, living or dead, business establishments, events, or locales is entirely coincidental.

In rural Malawi, a foreign aid worker is savagely killed by a mob of villagers. Investigating the grisly death, journalists Leo Bronson and Vivian Thomas uncover a heinous plot involving rumors, rage, and centuries-old superstition.

Rachel Woods entertains readers with her riveting mysteries, from cozies to whodunits. Now you can get one of her short stories for FREE, when you sign up to join her newsletter:

GET MY FREE SHORT STORY NOW

https://BookHip.com/PTTPAL

PROLOGUE

The bullet slammed into his gut ...

Aaron Jones cursed, staring at the dark, wet blood coating his palm. Blood on his hands. He'd been shot before he had a chance to beg for his life, but he had a feeling it wouldn't have mattered. His pleading would have fallen on deaf, unsympathetic ears. And why should he think he deserved any sympathy after what he'd done? The bullet in his gut was well earned. Still, he didn't want to die. Didn't want to bleed out like a stuck pig.

Struggling to breathe, panicked and fearful, Jones dropped to his knees near the bed and peered under the mattress. Gritting his teeth against the pain, he stared at the AR-15. The assault rifle was too far away, wedged between the metal frame under the bed. He could never get to it in time ...

Time. Was he running out? Did he have any left? Was time almost up for him?

Aaron Jones didn't want to die in a low-rent motel room that smelled like piss and furniture polish. Didn't want to breathe his last breath in Little Turkey, an impoverished neighborhood on the island of St. Killian.

Why was everything going straight to hell? How had things fallen apart? His plan hadn't been perfect, but it had been good enough to pull off.

Something had gone wrong.

His mind flew back in time to the beginning of the year, January, the month of resolutions, of putting the past behind, and resolving to move forth with new endeavors.

Jones recalled the day he'd received the first message:

I need you to look into something for me …

Had that been his first mistake?

Life was all about choices, and he'd made the wrong one when he found that damn letter. So many secrets in those words written so long ago. Instead of coming clean about what he knew, he'd decided to use the information to his advantage, for his own personal gain. And for what? What had his best-laid plans gotten him?

A bullet in the gut.

Forgetting about the gun, Jones tried to stand, but before he could get to his feet, a second bullet hit him, this time in the side.

"Wait …" Jones rasped, panic and pleading in his tone. "Please … don't—"

Another bullet put him on the ground, sprawled out on the thin, threadbare rug as his attacker stood over him, squeezing the trigger over and over, emptying the chamber.

Staring at the dirty, water-stained ceiling tiles, Jones lamented the mistakes he'd made, wished he'd made different decisions considering everything he knew …

The secrets he'd found out were devastating, life-changing … and extremely valuable.

Secrets in a blue file …

Jones coughed and tasted blood. Coughing again, he blinked rapidly as his vision blurred. He never should have trusted … but what did it matter now?

He raised a trembling hand and stared at the blood coating his palm.

No one would ever know the truth; no one would ever know that—

Blackness shrouded Aaron Jones, pulling him into a deep, dark void of nothingness …

1

"Beautiful afternoon for a wedding," whispered Vivian Thomas-Bronson. "Don't you think, Mr. Bronson?"

"I suppose," conceded her husband Leo, sounding as though he was reluctantly impressed. "If you like gorgeous sunset weddings in paradise."

The matrimonial ceremony of Derek Hennessy, the godson of Burt Bronson, Leo's dad, and Bessemer "Besi" Beaumont promised to be glamorous and poignant.

More than a hundred guests had gathered together on the private pink sand beach in front of Burt Bronson's mansion in Marchmont, the exclusive neighborhood on the north side of St. Killian, an island in the Palmchat Islands chain.

Local St. Killian glitterati joined some of the well-heeled wedding guests who'd flown down in advance of the weekend wedding. The combined wealth of the various wedding guests was probably more than the GDP of a small third-world country. From members of the Middle East ruling elite to the offspring of Wall Street wizards, the one percent was well represented, shining brighter than the diamonds that adorned fingers, necks, and wrists.

Derek, the son of the former Prime Minister of Canada, and Besi, an heiress to a grocery store fortune, were both childhood friends of Leo's. Although Leo took issue with the designation of Derek as a friend. Derek,

Besi and their wedding party of six had arrived on the island a week ago. Burt had promised to host the couple, and from the moment Derek had set foot on the island, Leo had been in a dour mood.

According to Leo, Derek Hennessy was his frenemy, an albatross around his neck. Vivian had been forced to listen to her husband's wild tales of debauchery and adventure he'd barely survived as he played the unwitting, and often unwilling, wingman to Derek.

There was the time when Derek lost a hundred thousand at an illegal poker game in Monte Carlo, and he and Leo had to run from Russian thugs. And the time when Derek got caught in Thailand with underage hookers and somehow Leo ended up in jail, where he might have stayed if not for the help of Burt's friend, the Canadian ambassador to Thailand.

Despite all that, Leo had agreed to be one of Derek's groomsmen. Reluctantly. And with some prodding from Vivian. Still, her husband had almost backed out after the wedding rehearsal dinner last night.

Tensions had run high. Alcohol combined with a game of "Never Have I Ever" had exposed deep-seated resentments between the wedding party members. There had been ugly accusations of cheating, tempers had flared, and the situation had nearly become physical.

In the end, the bride had kicked one of her bridesmaids—Winnie Quasebarth—out of the wedding.

Vivian had wondered if the wedding would be called off, but things had worked out.

Smiling, Vivian stood arm in arm with her husband at the beginning of the sandy path. Strewn with thousands of white hibiscus petals, it headed to the altar, a stunning pergola constructed of eight-foot potted palm trees. The wide fronds formed a natural arch over the bride and groom.

Several feet in front of Vivian and Leo were groomsman Tom York and bridesmaid Kelsea Gates. Tom, whose angular features and strong jaw were both appealing and anachronistic, looked like a matinee idol from the 1950s, with his exaggerated pompadour hairstyle and the pronounced cleft in his chin.

The daughter of a tech billionaire, Kelsea was tall and thin, with a Louise Brooks platinum blonde bob, an icy demeanor, and nonchalant attitude. She had high cheekbones, her best feature, and a small mouth drawn into a pucker, as though she was about to blow you a kiss ... or maybe spit in your face.

The pair walked in time to a Caribbean version of Pachelbel's "Canon in D" performed by a local steel drum band. Barefoot, they traversed the aisle first, passing between the rows of wedding guests who sat on bamboo chairs decorated with hanging bougainvillea. Vivian and Leo would head down the aisle next. Zeke Irving, the best man, would follow them, escorting Melanie Adams, the maid of honor.

"By the way, you look beautiful," whispered Leo. "Ravishing, actually."

"Like I could be ravished?" she asked, feeling the effects of his low timbre deep below her navel. "Or, like you want to ravish me?"

"Oh, I plan to ravish you," said Leo. "As soon as possible, and for a very long time."

The feeling below her navel intensified. Her cheeks aflame, she glanced away from Leo's salacious gaze. No use getting herself all hot and bothered when there was nothing they could do at the moment. Looking to her left, at the guests sitting on the bride's side, she focused on the well-dressed, well-heeled crowd and wondered if any of them would notice that Winnie Quasebarth was no longer in the wedding party.

After the brouhaha at the rehearsal dinner, Melanie came to the guest room where Vivian and Leo were staying with an urgent request. Her face blotchy from stress and tears, Melanie implored Vivian to take Winnie's place as a bridesmaid at the wedding. Sympathetic toward Melanie's distress at Besi's plight, Vivian had agreed without reluctance, but she'd pointed out that she didn't have a bridesmaid dress.

Melanie told her that the bridesmaid dress—a simple strapless dress made of silk and tulle—could be ordered and overnighted to the island in time for the wedding.

"Well, Mrs. Bronson," said Leo, his tone unenthusiastic. "Looks like it's our time to shine."

Vivian glanced toward the altar, where Tom and Kelsea had arrived and were taking their places. Recognizing their cue, Vivian nudged Leo, and they began their walk down the aisle. With the warm pink sand beneath her bare feet and the fading sunlight casting golden rays through the trees, Vivian couldn't help but reflect on her own wedding.

She and Leo had been married on the beach, but the ceremony had been much more intimate. They'd had a sunrise wedding, to signify the dawn of their new life together, and had invited a dozen close friends and family. Blessed with a gorgeous morning, their wedding had been magical and perfect—except for one thing.

Her best friend, Amal, had not been there to share Vivian's special day.

Vivian had chosen not to dwell on Amal's absence as she'd stood facing Leo, reciting her vows to him. She'd been overjoyed, and yet the moment was bittersweet. Amal would have been so thrilled for her.

Clutching her bouquet, a tropical mix of baby elephant leaves and small sego palms surrounded by vibrant bird of paradise, Vivian separated from Leo when they reached the altar.

With the wedding party in place, the guests stood, and minutes later, Besi walked down the aisle, resplendent, beautiful and glowing in a dazzling gown featuring hand-sewn Swarovski crystals.

Vivian couldn't help feeling sad for Besi, having neither of her parents present on her wedding day. Her father, grocery store magnate Samuel Beaumont, had a very advanced case of dementia and was being cared for by round-the-clock nurses. Unable to remember or comprehend one moment from the next, Samuel's prognosis was grim and had been hard on Besi, whose mother had died a year-and-a-half ago. Vivian had learned that Besi was an only child, as was her mother, Adrienne Elizabeth. Samuel's siblings were all dead, so she had no family at the wedding, unfortunately.

Despite not having her father to walk her down the aisle, Besi looked beautiful. Vivian recalled that one bridesmaid, Kelsea, believed Besi's looks had been improved by recent plastic surgery. Besi had visited the Aerie Islands months earlier to have a bump in her nose removed, possibly at Derek's request. When they were in prep school, Derek had teased Besi about her bump.

Taking her place in front of her groom, Besi took Derek's hands, and the ceremony began.

Following the minister's sermonizing about the sanctity and gravity of marriage, there was a Scripture reading, and then the minister led Derek through his vows, which he echoed with pompous confidence and arrogant entitlement. Vivian caught Leo's look of irritation and suppressed a laugh.

Glancing away from her husband, fearing she might expel an ill-timed giggle, Vivian focused on the audience, surveying the wedding guests.

At once, she realized she didn't see Derek's parents in the audience. Vivian had never met the former Canadian Prime Minister, but she'd seen lots of photos and video of David Hennessy and had no doubt she would recognize him, and Derek's mother, the glamorous former supermodel, Marcie Wallace. Why weren't they at the wedding?

As she scanned the guests, Vivian's gaze stopped on someone familiar.

Wearing dark sunglasses, a brunette woman, her hair pulled back in a tight chignon, perched on a chair on the very last row of the groom's side of the aisle. Was that Besi's good friend she'd met at the cocktail party six days ago? Vivian wasn't exactly sure, but she thought so.

Once Derek finished saying his vows, the minister instructed Besi to repeat after him. "I, Bessemer Elizabeth Beaumont, take thee, Derek Fitzpatrick Hennessy…"

Besi said, "I, Bessemer Elizabeth Beaumont, take thee, Derek Fitzpatrick Hennessy…"

The minister continued with the vows, and keeping with his instructions, Besi repeated, "… to be my wedded husband …"

Vivian sneaked a glance at the man she'd taken as her wedded husband. Her breath caught when she saw that Leo was staring at her, his look conveying his love. Was he thinking of their wedding day, too? Did he remember how special and magical it had been? Their joining had been miraculous. At one point in her life, Vivian had doubted that she would ever marry. Leo's aversion to marriage had torn them apart, but they'd found their way back to each other. Vivian vowed that nothing would ever split them apart again.

"To have and to hold from this day forward," intoned the minister.

Vivian gave Leo a small smile, and he gave her a look that exposed his thoughts. Her husband was thinking of ravishing her, and suddenly, Vivian couldn't wait. But first, Besi would have to finish her vows. And then Derek would have to kiss his new bride.

"For better or for worse," said the minister.

Following the pronouncement of Derek and Besi as man and wife, there would be the wedding processional, Vivian realized, and then photos of the wedding party. They would have to attend the reception, where Leo was scheduled to say a toast.

"For better or for worse," said Besi.

The minister said, "For richer and for poorer..."

As Besi repeated the vows, Vivian decided to forget about being ravished for the time being.

The minister said, "In sickness and in health, to love, cherish, and to obey, till death us do part..."

Glancing out at the audience, Vivian listened as Besi echoed the vows, "In sickness and in health, to love, cherish, and to obey, till death ..."

A loud gasp erupted, followed by exclamations of shock and horror.

Confused, Vivian turned back to the altar as a scream pierced the balmy air.

Crumpled at Derek's feet, Besi lay lifeless.

"Oh my God..." whispered Vivian, her hand pressed against her mouth as she stared at Besi, whose head was a pulpy, shattered mess of brain matter, scorched hair, and blood.

2

"Lemmie made you some hot tea," said Leo.

Adjusting the shawl around her bare shoulders, Vivian managed to smile as Leo walked into the library and headed to the couch where she sat with her leg tucked beneath her. She'd been in that same spot for an hour, since the police detectives had left the house to go back to the crime scene, where the cops would remain all night, collecting evidence.

Nearly eight hours had passed since Besi Beaumont had been killed. Vivian still couldn't shake the image of Besi lying in the sand, her wedding veil stained with splotches of brain and blood.

Accepting the mug from her husband, Vivian blew across the steaming surface, catching the faint smell of something fruity and sweet. "Is there lemon in the tea?"

Leo nodded as he sat next to her and pulled her into his arms. "And just a bit of rum."

Vivian took a cautious sip and savored the liquid, laced with distilled cane sugar, as it flowed down her throat and into her stomach. Despite the warmth of the tea, Vivian shivered in the bridesmaid dress she should have taken off hours ago.

Still shell-shocked and stunned, she felt paralyzed. Her mind in shambles, she struggled to make sense of what had happened to Besi. She couldn't believe Besi had been shot to death.

In the immediate aftermath of the horrific tragedy, Vivian had stood paralyzed, not sure if she should rush toward the scene to help Besi or stay back. Her mind flooded with terrorizing worry for Leo, and the safety of the bridal party and the wedding guests. Questions zipped through her head as screams and shouts intensified, rising to full-scale horror. Were they in the middle of an active shooter situation? Were they all easy, open targets? What was going on? How could this have happened? Why had it happened? Who would want to kill Besi? Was Besi the target? Or, an unintended victim? Where had the shot come from? Somewhere behind her? Oh, God … could she have been shot?

Sipping more of the tea, Vivian recalled how Derek, who stood unnervingly still as he stared down at Besi, was pushed aside by Tom York, who dropped to his knees in front of Besi and pulled her lifeless body into his arms. Rocking Besi's body back and forth, Tom wailed her name. When Derek tried to approach him, Tom snarled at Derek to stay away from Besi. Leo, Jacob, and Melanie rushed to Tom, pleading with him to release Besi's body so they could determine what had happened to her.

By that time, terror and confusion had spread through the crowd, more devastating than wildfire, devouring all sense of decency, common sense, and decorum.

"We're all going to die!"

"We need the police!"

"Call an ambulance!"

Panic spread quickly, undeterred and unrestrained after someone shouted that there was a sniper. Fearing for their lives, the guests scurried and scrambled, trampling over each other, racing toward a safe place to hide.

"How are you holding up, babe?" asked Leo, pressing his lips against her forehead.

"Okay, I guess," said Vivian, holding the mug with both hands. "I don't know. I'm still trying to process what happened, and I don't know how."

"Neither do I," said Leo. "One minute, I'm standing there waiting for the minister to pronounce Derek and Besi as husband and wife. The next, I'm watching Besi fall to the ground, and the back of her head is nothing but …"

Tears pricking her eyes, Vivian put the mug on the coffee table and then curled up next to Leo, pressing her face against the dress shirt he'd worn beneath his tuxedo, hiding in his strong arms wrapped around her.

"I'm surprised the two of you are still awake."

Wiping her eyes, Vivian moved away from Leo's embrace, staring at Burt as he strode toward them. Haggard and worn, his face was drawn and pale as he took a seat in one of the club chairs across from the couch.

"How's Derek?" asked Leo.

"Still in shock," said Burt. "He was given something to help him sleep. I just got off the phone with David. I hated having to give him such horrible news."

Vivian asked, "Are Derek's parents headed to the island?"

Burt hesitated, looking away, and then said, "I don't think so."

"Why not?" Leo asked.

Clearing his throat, Burt said, "I don't think David can clear his schedule."

"I don't understand. It was bad enough that he skipped the wedding," said Leo. "But his son's fiancée was shot dead during the ceremony. Doesn't he think that Derek needs his support?"

"We will support Derek in his father's absence," said Burt. "Now, more than ever, Leonard, is the time for you to truly set aside any bitterness you may still be harboring against Derek."

"Of course, I'm going to be there for Derek," said Leo.

Exhaling, Burt said, "The police are still at the crime scene, but they believe the bullet came from the trees."

"Do they think Besi was the target?" asked Leo. "Or was it a random shot?"

Vivian's stomach lurched. The idea of someone deliberately deciding to kill Besi on her wedding day was horrific, but a random, stray bullet meant that any member of the wedding party could have been killed. Panic threatened to overwhelm her as she realized that Leo could have been shot.

"They're not sure," said Burt. "I spent the last few hours meeting with the police chief, Detectives François and Janvier, and a team of policemen hand-picked by the chief. A task force has been formed to figure out how the hell this happened and find the bastard who killed Besi."

Leo nodded. "Let's hope the chief chooses Baxter François to lead the task force. He's the department's best detective."

Lips pursed, Burt pinched the bridge of his nose, and then said, "There's something else I need to discuss with both of you."

"What is it?" asked Vivian, her pulse jumping.

"As I'm sure you already know, considering that both Derek and Besi are from prominent, powerful families, the global press is descending," said Burt. "I've gotten word that correspondents from several cable news stations have already arrived on the island. I'm sure I don't need to tell you not to speak with the media."

"That's some kind of irony," said Leo.

Burt fixed them with a steely glare. "I do not want Derek or his family to become lurid tabloid fodder. And what happened to Besi is not to have any prominence in the *Palmchat Gazette*."

"You don't want to cover the story?" asked Vivian.

"The Associated Press ran a story they picked up from a stringer," said Burt. "It gives the basic facts without gory details or rampant speculation. We'll reprint that."

"The story is already trending, Dad," said Leo. "There have been a flood of requests for statements from Derek, and the wedding party, and the guests at the wedding."

"Leo and I have already gotten dozens of calls from colleagues all over the world," said Vivian. "Everyone wants to know—"

"I've been in touch with the head of publicity at Bronson Publishing to manage the interview requests," said Burt. "Statements on behalf of Derek and the wedding party, including yourself, are being crafted and will be disseminated to the media. As much as possible, I would like to shield Derek from the onslaught of the press. I hope I can count on your cooperation, Leonard."

"Are you sure this is the right way to handle this?" asked Leo. "Viv and I were first-hand witnesses, and we're friends of Derek. I'm sure that, together, we can create a poignant story that is both respectful and sensitive to Besi's memory and Derek's loss."

"Derek asked me to help him deal with the media, and that includes my publications as well," said Burt as he stood. "I have agreed to respect Derek's privacy during this shockingly horrific time, and I expect you to do the same and honor his wishes."

After Burt left the library, Leo turned to Vivian. "You think Dad's making the right decision?"

"Burt's probably right," said Vivian, remembering how she'd felt after losing her best friend. "Derek needs time to mourn."

When Amal had been murdered, Vivian hadn't wanted to talk to anyone. She could understand if Derek didn't want to share his pain or try to describe the depths of his sadness.

Nodding, Leo stood and then pulled Vivian to her feet. "We should probably try to get some rest."

Vivian agreed as she leaned against her husband, grateful for his strength as they left the library. But, she doubted she would sleep since she was afraid to close her eyes.

Each time she did, she saw Besi's white wedding veil splattered with blood.

3

After planting a kiss on Vivian's forehead, Leo slipped an arm around his wife's waist as they walked out of the guest room and down the wide hallway.

"Did you get any sleep?" asked Leo, feeling as though he'd only crawled into bed moments ago. Nevertheless, despite his exhaustion, he'd woken up around seven in the morning. He'd been wide awake, holding Vivian in his arms, staring at the tray ceiling above the bed when his cell phone vibrated. A text from Burt, informing him that a late morning breakfast had been arranged in the informal dining room for the wedding guests. Not that Leo thought anyone was in the mood to eat. His appetite was shot, and he was sure Vivian had little taste for anything beyond coffee and toast.

"Not really." Vivian leaned her head against his arm. "Every time I closed my eyes, I saw blood on a white veil."

"I think I was having crazy dreams," said Leo, unable to remember the bizarre images that had plagued his sleep.

"You were tossing and turning quite a bit," said Vivian.

"Didn't mean to keep you up, babe," Leo said, pulling her closer as they walked across the second-floor landing toward the curving staircase.

"You didn't keep me up," Vivian said. "Besi's murder kept me up. I couldn't stop thinking about it. I still can't. Who could have done something so horrible?"

Leo kissed his wife's forehead, disturbed by the unshed tears in the hoarseness of her voice.

"Hopefully, the cops will find out," said Leo.

"You think the task force is up to the challenge?" Vivian asked as they headed down the stairs. "Maybe the Palmchat Island Investigative Bureau should be called to help with the case?"

"I'm sure François and Janvier will call in reinforcements if they need them," said Leo.

"Detective François could ask his brothers for help," said Vivian.

"They're all detectives, right?" asked Leo, recalling that the François family was known for its inductive detection and investigative insight. Baxter François' grandfather and his father, both excellent lawmen, were famous for apprehending The Fury, a heinous serial killer with cannibalistic tendencies who'd stalked the islands more than twenty years ago.

"Three of them are," said Vivian.

"Thought Baxter had four brothers," said Leo as they turned right down the hall that led to the dining room.

"He does, but the youngest brother is still a—"

Glass shattered, followed by several high-pitched shrieks.

Leo tensed. "What the hell?"

"Something's going on in the dining room," said Vivian, her voice laced with apprehension. "We better see what's happening."

Following his wife down the hall, Leo entered the dining room and stopped.

Staring in shock, Leo winced as Derek slammed his fist into Tom's jaw, sending Tom sprawling back against the wall. On her feet, Melanie cried for Derek and Tom to stop fighting. Kelsea implored Zeke and Jacob to stop the men from killing each other. Cowering in their seats, neither Zeke nor Jacob seemed anxious to get into the middle of the fray.

"Leo, do something!" Vivian told him.

Hesitant to get involved, Leo took a few cautious steps into the dining room. "Derek! Tom! What the hell are you doing?"

"Leo! Thank God!" Kelsea ran over to him. "Make them stop fighting!"

"Why are they fighting?" asked Vivian. "What happened?"

"Tom was being an insensitive asshole," cried Kelsea, her face damp with tears. "He accused Derek of killing Besi!"

Groaning, Leo stared at Derek, who looked more like a raving maniac than a grieving groom as he stood in a fighting stance, fists raised, cursing and daring Tom to hit him.

Scrambling to his feet, Tom lurched toward the table, grabbed a fork, and turned to Derek.

"Oh, God, Tom, put that fork down!" Melanie yelled.

Brandishing the fork at Derek, Tom said, "Get back! Stay away from me, or I'll—"

Derek lunged at Tom, wrenching the fork from him and wrestling him to the floor. "You sonofabitch! How dare you say I killed Besi! How fucking dare you! I'll kill you!"

"Get off me!" Tom screamed, struggling to get away from Derek, who used his forearm to pin Tom to the floor. "You crazy murdering bastard!"

With a primal growl, Derek raised his free arm and stabbed the fork into Tom's cheek.

Kelsea's piercing scream was no match for Tom's wounded howl.

"Zeke! Jacob! A little help, please," requested Leo as he rushed toward Derek and Tom.

With Zeke's help, Leo managed to grab Derek and pull him away from Tom.

"Let me go!" Derek yelled, trying to yank free. "That asshole is not going to get away with what he said about me! Let me go!"

Jacob and Kelsea tended to Tom who held his cheek and whimpered, "He stabbed me! Crazy sonofabitch! He actually stabbed me!"

"You're lucky I didn't stab you in the heart!" said Derek as Leo, with Zeke's help, hustled him to the table and forced him to sit in one of the chairs.

"I'm lucky you didn't shoot me in the head!" countered Tom, rising to his feet, stumbling as he accepted a napkin from Kelsea to hold against his bloody face. "Like you did to Besi!"

Cursing, Derek jumped up, but Leo grabbed his shoulders and shoved him back into the chair. "Sit down and don't move! And, Tom, shut the hell up!"

"Derek killed her!" said Tom, glaring at Leo. "He didn't love her! He only wanted her money!"

"What in God's name is going on in here!"

Leo froze and saw that everyone else did, as well, as his father's commanding baritone boomed through the air. Even Derek lost some of his steam and slouched in his chair.

"Leonard," said his father, glaring at him. "What is the meaning of all this?"

Leaving Derek's side, Leo walked to his father. A feeling of déjà vu washed over him. Burt's stern gaze and the rebuke in his tone reminded Leo of all the times he'd gotten in trouble over something Derek had gotten him involved in.

"Tom and Derek got into it," said Leo, voice lowered. "But, it's going to be fine."

"Got into it how?" asked Burt, motioning for Leo to join him in the hallway, away from prying eyes and ears.

"Tom said something about Derek having to do something with Besi's murder," said Leo. "And then Derek took a swing at him."

"Tom is holding a bloody napkin against his face," said Burt, his gaze shifting from Leo to the scene in the dining room. "Derek seems to have done more than just take a swing at him."

Though it pained him to say it, Leo blurted out, "Derek stabbed Tom with a fork."

Burt exhaled and looked toward the ceiling. Focusing his gaze on Leo again, he said, "I'll handle this."

Relieved, Leo stepped aside, allowing his father to enter the dining room.

"Derek. Tom." Burt barked their names. "Both of you come with me. Now."

Looking like recalcitrant schoolboys sent to the headmaster's office, Derek and Tom left the dining room. Shoulders slumped and eyes averted, they gave each other a wide berth as they followed Burt.

Moments later, their faces somber and stunned, Melanie, Kelsea, Jacob, and Zeke said nothing as they drifted out of the dining room.

Sighing, Leo turned to Vivian, who walked toward him.

"Why would Tom accuse Derek of killing Besi?" asked Vivian. "You don't think it's true, do you?"

"No, babe, of course, it's not true," Leo said, deciding to ignore the sly sense of unease snaking through him.

4

"Guess what I get to do?" Leo strode into the breakfast nook, a large octagonal space off the kitchen, and sat in one of the twelve chairs positioned around the table.

"What?" Vivian glanced up from her iPad, where she'd been watching coverage of the Besi Beaumont murder on CNN, and muted the video.

"Bail Derek out of jail," Leo said, shaking his head as he reached for a muffin from the small buffet of breakfast offers on a large platter in the middle of the table. "Some fun, eh?"

"I can't believe Tom pressed charges," said Vivian, reaching for the coffee pot to pour Leo a cup of coffee.

"I can't believe anything that's happened," said Leo, sitting back in the chair. "I grew up with these people, and now I'm starting to wonder if I ever knew them at all."

"I'm sorry, sweetie," said Vivian, grabbing his hand. "I know how hard this is for you. I know what it's like to think you know someone and then realize that they were keeping secrets from you."

Leo's sympathetic smile lifted her spirits.

"I know you understand what I'm going through," said Leo. "Because of what you went through with Amal."

Sadness for the loss of her best friend welled within Vivian, but she willed herself not to cry.

"Amal was living a life that you knew nothing about," said Leo. "And that life got her killed. So, I can't help but wonder if Besi was keeping some secret that led to her death."

"It's not the secret that kills you," said Vivian. "It's that you know the secret."

"And if someone thinks you might tell the secret," said Leo, "they might kill you to stop that from happening."

"Let's not speculate until we have more information," said Vivian. "And speaking of that, I'm going down to the beach to see if Detective François will tell me how the investigation is going."

"Good luck with that," said Leo as he stood, and then kissed the top of her head.

"Good luck with Derek," said Vivian.

After Leo left to bail Derek out of jail, Vivian went back to their guest room to shower and change. An hour later, she left the mansion and headed down the path, taking the wooden-and-stone paver steps that winded down through the lush, dense jungle of flora and fauna to the boardwalk. Traversing the weathered planks, she hesitated as she approached the steps that led to the soft, pink sand.

Shuddering, Vivian stared at the beach, dotted with palm trees.

Two days ago, Besi Beaumont had walked down the aisle to marry a man she may, or may not, have loved, and instead had ended up with a bullet in the back of her head.

Vivian glanced toward the section of the beach where the ceremony had taken place.

The task force, a half-dozen members of the St. Killian police department, led by Detective Baxter François, walked among the wedding wreckage, stepping over broken bamboo chairs, the legs and backs snapped in half, and trampled flowers. Vivian thought it looked like the aftermath of a tropical storm. She understood that because the area was a crime scene, nothing could be moved, or cleaned up, so the scene wouldn't be disturbed. The police had to make sure that evidence was preserved so it could be collected and analyzed.

As balmy sea breeze blew across her face, Vivian stared at the pergola where Besi had lost her life.

Since the tragic events, she'd been trying to recreate the horrific scene in her mind, to determine if she may have seen something, anything, some clue or piece of evidence she could give to the police to help them find the person who'd shot Besi, but she hadn't been focused on the bride when the shooting had happened.

She'd been wrapped up in her own selfish thoughts about being ravished by Leo. Why hadn't she been paying attention to Besi? If she had, then maybe she would have seen …

Pushing the disturbing thoughts from her mind, Vivian walked over to Detective François, who was staring at his cell phone.

"Saw you on CNN this morning," said Vivian, forcing lightness into her tone, trying to combat the darkness threatening to overwhelm her spirit.

"Hope they got my good side."

Vivian laughed. The detective didn't have a bad side, but she didn't need to tell him that.

"Surprised you weren't there," he said. "Haven't seen much about the story in the *Palmchat Gazette*."

"You can blame the owner of the paper for that," said Vivian, lifting her braids and placing them over her right shoulder. "Derek is Burt's godson. He's family. Burt wants him protected, as much as possible."

"Yeah, we noticed the extra security," Baxter remarked.

"Burt hired them to keep the reporters and camera crews off his property," Vivian explained.

"We saw them camped out down at the far end of the beach," said Baxter. "But, I don't mind. The press just gets in the way, and we've got a hell of a lot of work to do to find whoever killed Ms. Beaumont."

"How's the investigation going?" asked Vivian, trying not to dwell on the fact that Besi had died before she had the chance to be declared Mrs. Hennessy.

"Not as well as I wish it were," remarked the detective. "Not as good as it will be when we find the killer."

"You got any leads?"

"None that I want reported in the *Palmchat Gazette*," said Detective François.

"I guess you're going to tell me the same thing you told CNN, huh?" asked Vivian, tilting her head. "Let's see if I remember the statement you gave at the press conference. The murder weapon was most likely a high-powered assault rifle. The police plan to view all the camera surveillance and are reaching out to the wedding guests for any cell phone video. At this time, there are no suspects, but you are following up on several promising leads."

"That's about all I have to say," said the detective, smiling at her.

"Well, if there is something you want to tell me that you didn't tell CNN, feel free," said Vivian. "Leo's dad doesn't want us to cover the story, out of respect for Derek's tragic loss."

The detective stared at her. "So, if I tell you something, I won't have to worry about reading it online?"

Shaking her head, Vivian said, "Not this time."

"Well, in that case," said the detective. "We believe we know exactly where, in the trees, the shooter was hiding when Ms. Beaumont was fired upon and killed. Several strands of dark brown hair were caught on some of the tree branches."

"Male or female hair?" asked Vivian.

"Still waiting on forensics to let me know," said François.

"And when forensics lets you know, will you let me know?" asked Vivian, though she suspected she knew what his answer would be.

"How about I let you know this," said the detective. "Also found in the trees was a piece of fabric."

"What kind of fabric?" Vivian asked, glancing over her shoulder toward the tree line of sea grape trees that bordered the lush vegetation clustered on the storied slope rising toward Burt's massive mansion on the bluff above the sea.

"Peach-colored silk," said Detective François. "Looked like it had been ripped from a pretty fancy dress."

"Peach-colored?" asked Vivian. "Like the bridesmaid's dresses we wore?"

"That's right, you were in the wedding," said the detective, giving her his sexy smile. "I saw you on one of the videos. You looked nice."

Ignoring the detective's compliment, she said, "Do you think the fabric came from a bridesmaid dress?"

"From the video I've seen of the ceremony, it certainly appears as though the piece of fabric we found in the trees might be the same type of fabric that those bridesmaids dresses were made from. We'll need forensics to examine the dresses. One of the deputies will be contacting you and the two other bridesmaids to get the dresses. First thing we need to do is determine if the fabric we found matches the fabric from the bridesmaid dresses. Again, from the video I saw, seemed like a lot of the guests were wearing peach."

"Besi wanted the wedding guests to wear colors of the sunset," said Vivian.

"I'm sure we'll be able to rule the bridesmaids out as suspects," said Baxter.

"How are you so sure?" asked Vivian.

"Doesn't make sense that one of the bridesmaids fired a shot from thirty, maybe forty feet away while they were standing inches away from the bride."

"True, but ..." Vivian glanced toward the pergola. Beyond the palm trees, near the edge of the beach, gentle waves lapped against the pink sand.

"But ..." the detective prompted.

Disturbed by what she was going to tell the detective, Vivian sighed. "I know how one of the bridesmaids could have fired that shot from forty feet away."

Detective François frowned. "How?"

"The bridesmaid could have fired the shot because she wasn't a bridesmaid."

Shaking his head, the detective said, "I don't understand."

Vivian said, "Winnie Quasebarth was supposed to be a bridesmaid, but she was kicked out of the wedding the day before the ceremony. That's how I ended up in the wedding. I took Winnie's place."

"Why was she kicked out of the wedding?"

Vivian hesitated, wishing she hadn't said anything about Winnie before talking to Leo.

"Mrs. Bronson?"

"Winnie argued with Besi," said Vivian, though calling what transpired between Besi and Winnie an argument was a blatant understatement. Winnie had accused Derek of cheating on Besi. The future Mrs. Derek Hennessy wasn't in the mood for any aspersions cast against her man.

Lunging at Winnie, Besi had grabbed the mining heiress around the throat. Chaos ensued as Besi went full-on bridezilla, punching and slapping Winnie, who held her own with a few well-placed kicks. Derek, Tom, Leo, and Zeke desperately tried to separate the women while Kelsea, Melanie, and Jacob begged the friends to stop fighting.

"And it got very intense," Vivian went on, "and Besi kicked Winnie out the wedding."

His gaze circumspect, the detective said, "So, this Winnie Quasebarth has beef with the bride, gets kicked out of the wedding, and then the next day, at the wedding Winnie was kicked out of, the bride is shot dead. Interesting …"

5

"Are you serious?" Leo stared at his father, not sure he'd heard him correctly.

"I don't understand," said Vivian, sitting next to him.

"I could not be more serious if I tried, Leonard," his father thundered from behind the massive desk in his cavernous office.

"Dad, start from the beginning, please, " Leo requested as he sat forward in the antique chair.

"I don't know how to make it any plainer," said Burt, sighing as he slumped back in his leather chair. "I got a call from the chief of police, who informed me that Winnie Quasebarth confessed to the murder of Besi."

"That doesn't make any sense," said Leo, dragging a hand down his jaw. "How the hell could Winnie have killed Besi? Winnie was kicked out of the wedding."

"What evidence do the police have against her?" Vivian asked.

"I doubt they have any evidence against her," said Burt, his frown deepening. "Her confession is obviously some misguided attempt to get Derek's attention. The police never should have taken her claims seriously. She should not be in jail."

The idea of Winnie killing Besi was farfetched, despite Winnie's crazy outburst at the rehearsal party or the conversation Vivian had with Winnie.

Leo was fairly certain that Winnie wasn't a murderer, but why would she confess to killing Besi if she hadn't done it?

"Winnie is a fragile girl," said Burt. "She's experiencing some mental trauma and should not be used as a scapegoat just because the police want to close the case and keep it out of the media."

"You think the cops would accept a false confession just to say they solved Besi's murder?" Leo asked.

Burt said, "This is a high-profile case, one which could negatively affect tourism. It is in the best interest of the St. Killian PD to make a quick arrest."

"Have the police considered that Winnie might not have been physically able to kill Besi?" asked Vivian. "Detective François told CNN that the murder weapon was likely a high-powered assault rifle. I doubt Winnie would be able to handle a gun like that."

Leo said, "Actually, Winnie is an accomplished shooter. She did pistol and rifle shooting competitions at school. That's how she, Besi, and Kelsea became friends. Winnie was trained by Australian special forces. Alfred Quasebarth hired a former sniper so Winnie could crush the competition."

"Despite Winnie's proficiency with firearms, I still do not believe she killed Bessemer," said Burt. "I would like you to prove that, Leonard."

Leo gaped at his father. "How the hell am I supposed to do that?"

"If Winnie didn't kill Besi," said Vivian, "then the police shouldn't find any evidence against her."

"I'm afraid Winnie might try to incriminate herself to prove her guilt," said Burt. "For that reason, Leonard, I am hoping you can prove her innocence."

"Dad," Leo began, hoping his rising frustration wouldn't hamper his attempt to convince Burt to listen to reason and abandon the idea of making him investigate. "Baxter François is a great detective, and Janvier is pretty okay, too. I'm sure that the two of them, together, will be able to determine the veracity of Winnie's claims."

Burt exhaled. "Leonard, please do not try my patience about this."

Grumbling, Leo capitulated.

"Now with that settled, if the two of you wouldn't mind giving me a bit of privacy, I'd appreciate it," said Burt. "I have to call Alfred Quasebarth, and I'm sure it's going to be a difficult conversation."

"Of course," said Vivian, standing.

Leo stood, grabbed his wife's hand, and guided her out of his father's office.

Walking down the wide hallway back toward their guest room, Leo asked, "Why the hell would Winnie confess to killing Besi?"

"Do you believe her?" asked Vivian.

Leo exhaled. "Winnie didn't kill anybody. François and Janvier will figure that out."

"Burt wants you to do it," reminded his wife.

Leo dragged a hand along his jaw. "Yeah, but—"

Abruptly, Vivian faced him, halting their progress down the hallway.

"Babe, what is it?" asked Leo, worried by his wife's pained expression.

Vivian said, "I think we should prove that Winnie is innocent."

"I think we should let the cops handle it," said Leo. "Or, better yet, let the Quasebarth legal department deal with Winnie's crazy confession."

"But, it's my fault that she confessed," Vivian blurted out, averting her gaze.

Leo asked, "How is it your fault?"

"You remember I told you about my conversation with Detective François?" asked Vivian. "He told me the cops found a torn piece of peach-colored fabric in the trees heading up toward the bluff."

Leo nodded. "That's why the police are going to check all the bridesmaids' dresses. They need to rule out you, Melanie, and Kelsea as suspects."

"What I didn't tell you is that I told Baxter François that Winnie got kicked out of the wedding," said Vivian. "When she left the house and headed to the Queen Palm hotel, I think she took everything with her—including her bridesmaid dress."

Confused, Leo asked, "You think Winnie put on her bridesmaid dress to hide in the trees and shoot Besi?"

"What I mean is," said Vivian, taking a deep breath. "Detective François probably wouldn't have questioned Winnie if I hadn't told him that she was kicked out of the wedding for arguing with Besi."

"You don't know that François wouldn't have questioned Winnie," said Leo, pulling his wife into his arms and kissing her forehead. "And just because the cops questioned Winnie didn't mean she had to confess to something she probably didn't do."

"You're probably right," said Vivian, standing on her toes to kiss him. "But, I would feel better if we tried to help Winnie."

Leo sighed and smiled at the love of his life. "How do you suggest we start this informal investigation into Besi's murder?"

"We should talk to the wedding party," said Vivian. "Remember my friend, Octavia Constant?"

"The defense attorney?"

"She told me once that the key to her success is that she looks for a better suspect," said Vivian. "She finds the person who had a better motive to kill the victim than her client. That's what we need to do. We have to find out if someone—besides Winnie—wanted Besi dead."

6

"Kelsea?" Vivian knocked on the half-opened door before she entered Kelsea Gates' guest room. "Do you have a minute to—"

"Actually, no, I don't have a minute," said Kelsea, throwing clothes into the Vuitton suitcase on the bed. "I have a plane to catch in an hour."

"You're leaving?" asked Vivian, glad she'd opted for a quick breakfast. If she'd lingered over goat cheese scones and coffee, Kelsea might have left the mansion before she had a chance to question her.

"Getting the hell off 'murder island' before I get shot in the head by some random wacko."

"You think some random stranger killed Besi?" asked Vivian, walking toward the bed table. "You don't think Besi was killed by someone who knew her or specifically targeted her?"

"For all I know, we might all be fucking targets." Kelsea stomped to the large wardrobe in the corner where she yanked several dresses from their silk-covered padded hangers. Stomping across the room back to the bed, she dropped the dresses into the suitcase.

"Who might be targets?"

"Everybody in that whacked out wedding party," said Kelsea, making another trip to the wardrobe. "Some psycho might be trying to kill all of us!"

"For what reason?" asked Vivian, wondering if Kelsea's speculation was a valid concern or unfounded paranoia.

Glaring at Vivian, Kelsea rolled her eyes. "How the hell should I know?"

Vivian took a deep breath. "I know you're busy, and I don't want to take up too much of your time, but ..."

Kelsea stalked to the dresser, yanked it open and scooped out a pile of lacy underwear.

Clearing her throat, Vivian said, "If it turns out that Besi wasn't killed by a random person, then do you have any idea who might have wanted to kill her?"

Stopping in the middle of the bedroom, her arms loaded with designer duds, Kelsea stared at Vivian, eyes narrowed. "Why are you asking me that?"

"I was just wondering because—"

"Because you're a reporter," said Kelsea, as though the word, 'reporter' was something sour in her mouth. "You work for Mr. Bronson's newspaper. Are you trying to get a quote from me on the sly? I don't have a fucking thing to say to the media, and that includes the *Palmchat Gazette,* and you aren't supposed to be interviewing me because Leo's father said—"

"No, no, Kelsea, I'm not trying to interview you," said Vivian, hoping to put the irate heiress at ease. "I'm not asking as a reporter."

"Then why are you asking?" asked Kelsea, frowning. "I already talked to the police."

"I'm asking on behalf of Leo's father," said Vivian, realizing she had to bring out the big guns, and leverage Burt's influence. "He wants me and Leo to find out who might have wanted Besi dead."

"How would I know who wanted Besi dead?" asked Kelsey. "All I know is that I didn't."

"Did the police ask you if you'd had anything to do with Besi's murder?"

Kelsey rolled her eyes. "Can you believe they had the actual balls to ask me that ridiculous question? Why the hell would I want to kill Besi?"

"Maybe you wanted to get rid of your rival," suggested Vivian.

Kelsey frowned. "My rival?"

"For Derek's affections," said Vivian. "You were having an affair with him, right?"

Kelsey rolled her eyes again. "An affair? Are you serious right now?"

"Mr. Bronson's house manager, Lemuel Shaw," began Vivian, "confided in me that he caught you and Derek ... together ... in the laundry room."

"Does Leo's dad know that the help is gossiping about his guests?" asked Kelsey, resuming her frantic packing.

"So it's not true?" asked Vivian. Staring at the icy heiress, she thought about the bridesmaid's dalliance with the groom. Lemmie had caught them in the spacious industrial laundry room. Kelsea had been bent over one of the dryers and Derek had been behind her, with his pants around his ankles. With several laundry machines going at the same time, Lemmie didn't think he'd been noticed, though he'd done a hasty about-face as soon as he'd realized what was happening.

Shrugging, Kelsey said, "So Derek and I hooked up once or twice? It was no big deal. Derek just needed to relieve some stress."

"He was stressed about the wedding?" asked Vivian.

Kelsey's forehead wrinkled. "I don't think so. Something else was on his mind. I don't know what. And I didn't care. Anyway, as for who wanted Besi dead, I heard Winnie confessed." "No one believes that Winnie killed Kelsea."

Shrugging, Kelsea said, "Maybe they should."

"Why do you say that?" Vivian asked. "Do you suspect Winnie?"

"She's batshit bonkers," Kelsey said, rolling her eyes. "She's probably capable of anything—even killing Besi."

"Did you tell the police that?" asked Vivian.

"Winnie's a psycho, but she's still my friend," Kelsey said, sinking onto the settee at the foot of the bed. "I don't want to get her in trouble."

"What do you mean?" Vivian questioned, joining Kelsea on the settee. "How could you get Winnie in trouble?"

Kelsea sighed, shaking her head. "Winnie sent me a text. I thought it was crazy, but ..."

"What did the text say?"

"I'll show you." Kelsea rose from the settee and walked to the sitting nook in the corner, where a pink Birkin bag sat on the small table positioned between two chairs. Fishing in the purse, Kelsea pulled out a cell phone. After rejoining Vivian on the settee, Kelsea handed her the phonc.

Taking the phone, Vivian read: *That bitch doesn't deserve Derek! I'll kill her before I let her have him!*

Glancing at Kelsea, Vivian asked, "When did she send this to you?"

"Saturday morning," Kelsea said. "The day of Derek's and Besi's wedding."

7

"Dead guy found at the Flamingo Inn motel was named Aaron Jones," said Sophie, reading notes from her smartphone.

Following the conversation with Kelsea Gates earlier that morning, Vivian had left the mansion in her Range Rover and headed to the *Palmchat Gazette* offices. During the drive, Sophie had texted Vivian concerning a story.

Dead body found @ motel n Little Turkey. Cops think homicide. Want me 2 cover it since Beanie's on a story in Handweg.

Vivian had dispatched Sophie to the scene to get details and was now being debriefed.

Grabbing a red editing pen from the mug she used as a pencil holder, Vivian focused on Sophie, sitting in one of the chairs in front of the desk.

The junior reporter, who'd graduated from college with a journalism degree two years ago, was ambitious and tenacious, but Sophie had an attention span problem. Sometimes, she didn't ask the right questions or get the most pertinent information to ensure that she told the best story, one that was both interesting and contained all the facts known at the time. As a result, Vivian often had to instruct her to go back to the scene of the crime, so to speak, for more details. With the proper guidance, however, Vivian was certain she could mold Sophie into a top-notch investigative reporter.

"Cops think he was a tourist," said Sophie. "They found his passport in the motel room. That's how they identified him."

"How was he killed?" Vivian asked, though her mind wandered back to the text Kelsea had shown her. Winnie had threatened to kill Besi to stop her from marrying Derek. The message, sent before the doomed wedding, was disturbing, but could it be taken seriously? Should it be?

Sophie said, "He was shot to death. Cops are doing ballistics on the bullet, but Officer Fields said they think it was a small caliber handgun. Maybe a .22 or a .38. That's not all they found."

As Sophie continued, Vivian wondered if Winnie was capable of putting a bullet in Besi's head. The last time she'd seen Winnie, the mining heiress had been spitting mad, cursing and fighting, drunk and belligerent. But, had that violent behavior become homicidal rage?

"That's why the police think he was leaving the island," said Sophie.

Realizing she hadn't been listening, Vivian stared at Sophie. "What? Say that again, please?"

"The cops think the dead tourist, Aaron Jones, was leaving the island in a few days," said Sophie.

"How do they know that?"

"They found an airline eTicket in his duffle bag," said Sophie. "Did I forget to mention that?"

"Sorry, Sophie," said Vivian, feeling sheepish. "I was half-listening. I tuned out when you were telling me about the other things the police found in Aaron Jones' motel room."

"You okay?" asked Sophie. "You want to talk about this later?"

"No, I want to hear about it now," said Vivian, resolved to move on from her contemplation of Winnie's homicidal tendencies. "Seems like it'll be a good story for you and you've gotten some good details."

Smiling, Sophie said, "Okay, so the cops also found money stuffed in an expensive Hermes leather briefcase."

"How much money?" asked Vivian, her interest in the story growing.

Eyes alive with excitement, Sophie said, "A hundred thousand dollars."

Vivian tapped her editing pen against her cheek. "Do the cops have any suspects?"

Sophie's face fell. "I forgot to ask about suspects."

Vivian suppressed her frustration.

"I'll call Detective François and ask him," said Sophie.

"Baxter François likes to keep his thoughts to himself unless you have something to give him," said Vivian, her tone a bit more curt than she intended. "Even when he tells you something, he never wants to be quoted."

Sighing, Sophie nodded. "Everything's always off the record with him."

"Call Officer Fields instead," said Vivian, who'd been working on developing a good rapport with St. Killian cops who seemed more amenable to sharing information. "And ask him about a motive, too."

After Sophie left her office, Vivian thought about Aaron Jones' murder. Robbery wasn't the motive. His killer hadn't taken the Hermes briefcase, which was easily worth ten thousand dollars, or the money. Why not? Maybe the killer hadn't known there was money in the duffle bag? Or, maybe the killer didn't care. Maybe the killer just wanted Aaron Jones dead.

8

Leo walked toward the pool, where Tom York, dressed in rumpled slacks and a wrinkled dress shirt and wearing sunglasses, slouched on a chaise beside the pool.

Reluctant, Leo approached Tom, not sure what state of mind he might be in.

An hour ago, Leo had spoken with Zeke and Jacob. Neither of them had much more to say other than they were still reeling from the tragic events at the wedding. Not surprisingly, they had no idea who might have killed Besi and couldn't imagine that she had any enemies.

Now, faced with asking Tom those same questions, Leo felt irate and irritated.

Tom's unadulterated grief after Besi's murder bothered Leo. But he wasn't surprised. Tom and Besi had been having an affair behind Derek's back. Leo had caught Tom and the bride having a lover's spat several days before the wedding.

When confronted, Besi had denied being in love with Tom. She'd claimed their dalliances hadn't mattered. Their hookups had been a mistake she regretted.

Figuring he wouldn't get much more from Tom than he'd learned from

Zeke and Jacob, Leo strode toward Tom, deciding to ask him a few questions and then get on with more important things.

"Hey, Tom," said Leo, easing down onto the chaise next to Tom.

Turning his head toward Leo, Tom mumbled an unintelligible response.

"How you holding up?" asked Leo, his gaze dropping to the four empty Felipe beer bottles beneath Tom's chaise.

Saying nothing, Tom stared straight ahead, his jaw clenched.

Pinching the bridge of his nose, Leo tried to ignore the annoyance rising in his chest. Focused on his task and getting it over and done with as quickly as possible, he said, "Seems like it's been pretty rough on you."

Tom shrugged.

Leo tried another tactic. "I didn't know you and Besi were so close."

"We were more than close," said Tom, a defensive edge to his tone.

"What does that mean?" asked Leo, hoping to get some clarity on Tom's and Besi's relationship. "Just how close were you and Besi?"

"How close do you think we were?" Tom snarled. "You saw us together."

"I heard you saying some threatening things to her," said Leo. "And I heard her trying to get away from you."

"I wasn't threatening her," said Tom. "I was reminding her how much we mean to each other."

"Maybe the two of you didn't mean as much as you thought," said Leo.

Tom sat up and turned his head toward Leo. "Besi and I loved each other."

"And yet she was going to marry Derek," said Leo, wishing Tom would lose the dark sunglasses. A low cloud deck had moved over the island, threatening rain and obscuring the sun, so there was no need for the shades.

"What do you want, Leo?" Tom asked. "I doubt you give a shit about how I'm doing."

Bristling, Leo bit back an angry retort and instead said, "I'm not trying to upset you, Tom. I want to ask you some questions about Besi's murder. You have any idea who might have wanted to kill her?"

"Winnie," said Tom.

Confused, Leo asked, "You think Winnie killed Besi?"

"She confessed, didn't she?"

"But why did you accuse Derek?" Leo asked. "That's why the two of you were fighting. You said Derek was responsible for Besi's murder."

Tom swung his legs off the chaise, yanked the sunglasses from his eyes, and glared at Leo. "Derek's relationship with Besi made Winnie snap. Derek is the reason why Besi is dead."

"Why do you say that?" asked Leo.

"It's like I told those island cops, not that they believed me," said Tom, "but Derek was only marrying Besi for her money."

"Derek has money," Leo reminded him. "His family is just as wealthy as Besi's."

Tom snorted. "Just because Derek's family has money doesn't mean that Derek has money."

Leo shook his head. "I don't understand."

"Derek got fired from Hennessy Capital," said Tom.

"I thought he left his dad's company," Leo said.

Tom scoffed. "He was told to leave."

"Why?"

Shrugging, Tom said, "Not sure. Derek was evasive, trying to make it seem as though parting ways was a mutual decision. My guess? David Hennessy was sick of Derek doing more gambling than working."

"You know a guy named Skip Taylor?" asked Leo, remembering a question he'd forgotten to ask Zeke and Jacob. "Has a heavy New Jersey accent. Looks like DeNiro when he played Al Capone in *The Untouchables*."

Tom shook his head. "Never heard of him. Who is he?"

"Friend of Derek's," said Leo. "I overheard Derek and this Skip guy talking in the library last week."

"About what?"

"Some problem Derek needed help with," said Leo, recalling the conversation. "Something about money. Derek told Skip to make the problem go away."

Tom scoffed. "Probably some problem with a bookie Derek owes money but won't pay."

Leo glanced toward the pool. Could the conversation he'd overheard between Derek and Skip Taylor been about a gambling debt? Maybe Skip had to fix a problem with a bookie who insisted that Derek settle his accounts.

Letting out a long breath, Tom said, "Derek wasn't in love with Besi. He wasn't faithful to Besi, and he didn't give a shit about Besi. Wacko Winnie lost her mind when she found out Derek had proposed to Besi instead of her."

Jarred by Tom's jump to another subject, Leo asked, "Derek had something going on with Winnie?"

Tom ran his hands down the back of his head. "No, but the way Winnie figured it, if Derek wanted to marry a rich girl that he didn't love, then he should have chosen her. Instead, Derek chose Besi and Winnie freaked out. You saw yourself, at the rehearsal dinner, how jealous Winnie was of Besi. She couldn't stand the thought of Derek marrying Besi."

Unconvinced by Tom's theory, Leo said, "You think Winnie killed Besi in a jealous rage?"

"I don't think it, I know it," said Tom. "And you know what else I know? Derek had his choice between Besi and Winnie. If he had chosen Winnie, then Besi would still be alive."

9

Sitting on the pool level of Burt's mansion, under the shaded portion of the terrace, Vivian stared at the screen of her laptop.

Minutes ago, Sophie had texted Vivian, asking if she was coming into the office. Vivian responded that she planned to head to the *Palmchat Gazette* after lunch. Sophie wanted to speak with her about a potential story, so Vivian had decided to facilitate a Skype video call. She didn't want to dampen Sophie's enthusiasm, especially if the story was worthy of prominent placement in the newspaper.

"What's your story idea?" asked Vivian, refocusing the conversation to the reason for the video call.

"Stevie was manning the police scanner last night," began Sophie, referring to Stevie Bishop, another junior reporter at the paper. "There was a call about a guy lying in a ditch, and at first the police thought he'd had a heart attack, but he'd been shot."

Slightly interested, Vivian said, "You have any other details?"

"The victim is in the hospital, but he's not available to give a statement because he's in a coma," said Sophie. "The motorist who accidentally hit the man stopped to render aid, so the cops probably won't be charging him."

"At least it wasn't a hit and run," said Vivian, willing herself not to dwell on the similarities between what had happened to last night's victim and her best friend's heinous, senseless murder. Amal had been hit by a car, run down in the middle of the night by a twisted psychopath.

"Guess there's not that much to the story." Sophie exhaled. "You think it's worth pursuing?"

"Where was he found?"

"Oyster Farms," said Sophie.

"Really?" asked Vivian, her interest growing. Oyster Farms, a working-class neighborhood, was known for its modest homes, well-kept lawns, and quiet streets. The residents were by no means wealthy, but they made a decent living and made a point to live peaceable lives.

"There's not much crime in Oyster Farms," said Vivian.

"That's why I was thinking it might be worth pursuing the story," said Sophie. "Who knows? Maybe the guy was shot somewhere else and then dropped off in Oyster Farms."

"Maybe," said Vivian. "See what you can find out and email me the first draft in a few hours."

"Great!" Sophie smiled. "I'll get right on it."

"Before you go," said Vivian. "Good job on the Little Turkey motel murder story."

Sophie beamed. "Thanks! I just wish I could have gotten more information about a motive."

"You did find out that there are no suspects at this time," said Vivian. "Make sure you keep in contact with Officer Fields for any updates."

After ending the video call with Sophie, Vivian closed her laptop, leaned back against the couch cushions, and rubbed her eyes. She was proud of Sophie for her aggressive pursuit of some very interesting stories. Unfortunately, Vivian feared that no one would be interested in reading them. The entire Palmchat Island chain was riveted by the murder of Besi Beaumont and residents were rabid for news about the story. Because of Burt's decision not to cover the story out of respect for Derek's privacy, the *Palmchat Gazette* had suffered some of its lowest traffic numbers, according to the online data metrics reports. People wanted to read about Besi Beaumont, and if they couldn't get the news they craved from the *Palmchat Gazette*, then they would get their fix from other publications.

Staring toward the pool, watching the sunlight dance on the water,

Vivian contemplated a plan to make up the online traffic deficiency. The *Palmchat Gazette* needed an exclusive, explosive story related to the Besi Beaumont murder. She needed to convince Burt to let her interview Derek Hennessy and the rest of the wedding party. If she could explain to Burt that his decision was negatively affecting the bottom line, then maybe—

"Excuse me, Vivian."

Jumping slightly, Vivian glanced over her shoulder.

Melanie Adams, her face drawn, pale, and blotchy, stood behind the couch. "Sorry. I didn't mean to startle you."

"No, it's fine," said Vivian. "I was just lost in thought."

"Mr. Shaw said you wanted to talk to me," said Melanie, fingers curled around the ends of a shawl wrapped around her hunched shoulders. "I'm sorry I wasn't available yesterday. I just haven't been up to talking to anyone about anything after I spoke with the police."

"I understand," said Vivian as Melanie walked around the couch and sat down.

"What did you need to talk to me about?"

Vivian hesitated. Melanie looked so forlorn and despondent. Vivian didn't want to upset her with questions about Besi's death, and if not for Burt's request, she would have forgone the inquiry.

"I hate to ask you this," said Vivian, pausing before she went on. "But, Burt wanted me and Leo to find out if there is any possibility that Winnie could have hurt Besi."

Twisting the ends of the shawl into a knot, Melanie stared at her. "You mean, is Winnie's confession real? I don't think so. I doubt it."

"Kelsea showed me a text from Winnie that said—"

"That Winnie would kill Besi over Derek?" Melanie rolled her eyes. "Kelsea showed me that text."

"You weren't bothered by it?" Vivian asked.

Melanie said, "Winnie is always threatening to kill people over some perceived slight or offense. It's sort of her thing. No one takes her seriously."

"Do you think you should have taken Winnie seriously?" asked Vivian.

"Maybe I should have." Melanie exhaled. "Maybe if I had taken Winnie seriously, then maybe Besi wouldn't be dead."

Vivian shook her head. "You can't blame yourself."

"Why shouldn't I?" asked Melanie, her face a mask of despair. "I was Besi's assistant, her maid of honor. I should have protected her. Should have made sure she was okay. I owed her that. I owe Besi so much. She was the best friend I ever had. She was the only one who was always nice to me when we were in school. I wasn't rich like her, or Derek, or Leo, or Kelsea. My dad was a teacher, and that's how I ended up going to school with the rich and famous. And trust me when I tell you that the trust fund babies let me know that F. Scott Fitzgerald was right about the rich being different. The super rich are even worse."

Vivian nodded, saying nothing, deciding to let Melanie fill the silence.

"Besi wasn't like that, though," said Melanie. "Her family had billions, but she never tried to make me feel inferior because I didn't have money or social status. She was always so nice to me. She defended me. She accepted me and included me. I can't believe that she's gone, and she's never coming back."

Melanie's quiet sobs pricked Vivian's heart, reminding her of her loss, and she said, "I know how you feel."

Wiping her eyes, Melanie looked confused. "What?"

"I lost my best friend, too," said Vivian, praying she could keep the tears at bay. "She was murdered."

"Oh, God, I'm so sorry," said Melanie, her expression pained.

Pushing away the depressing thoughts, Vivian took a deep breath. "Do you have any idea who might have wanted to hurt Besi?"

Looking away, Melanie twisted the ends of the shawl together.

"That's all I've been doing since she was shot," said Melanie, glancing at Vivian. "Trying to think of who wanted to hurt her. And, actually, I think I know who might have killed Besi."

10

"And you think this guy killed Besi?" Vivian asked ten minutes later, as she and Melanie sat in the sitting area of the guest bedroom Melanie had been assigned.

Exhaling, Melanie removed the shawl, rolled it into a ball, and placed it on the small table between the two winged back chairs they sat in.

"I don't know for sure," said Melanie. "I think it's possible, but ..."

Vivian exhaled, trying to temper her disappointment. "But you don't know the guy's name."

"I have no idea who he is," said Melanie. "That's why I didn't tell the cops about him. I want to give the police evidence they can use. I want to give them more than just speculation or conjecture. I want to give them something that leads to the killer, but all I know is that some guy was harassing Besi. He was sending her threatening emails."

"But, you never saw the emails, right?" Vivian asked, confirming what Melanie had told her moments before.

Shaking her head, Melanie said, "Besi just told me about the emails."

"When did the guy send Besi the threatening emails?"

"Maybe about six months ago," said Melanie.

After quick calculations in her head, Vivian said, "That would have been around February."

Nodding, Melanie said, "I'd forgotten about those emails until yesterday when I was getting Besi's things together. I came across her phone. It was beeping, signaling that she had messages and emails. So, I checked the messages, and then—"

"How did you check the messages?" asked Vivian. "Wasn't Besi's phone password protected?"

"As her assistant, I have the password to her phone," said Melanie. "Derek used to have the passwords until Besi asked me to change them."

Vivian asked, "Why did Besi want you to change her passwords?"

"When she was in the Aerie Islands to get her surgery," said Melanie. "I got a call from the Rakestraw Blake Center saying that Besi had missed her appointment."

"Besi didn't get the surgery?"

"No, she did," said Melanie. "I called her after the Rakestraw Blake Center called me—I was listed as her emergency contact—and she told me that someone stole her purse, with all her credit cards and identification and her passport. She missed the surgery because she was at the police station filing a complaint," said Melanie. "Anyway, she rescheduled the surgery. But, she was afraid her accounts would be hacked, so she told me to change all the passwords."

"Let's go back to the threatening messages Besi received six months ago," said Vivian. "I know you didn't see the emails but did Besi tell you what they said?"

Reaching for the shawl again, Melanie said, "Besi said the guy was hounding her about meeting with him. He would tell her not to ignore him and said that she would lose everything if she refused to meet with him."

"So, he didn't threaten to kill Besi?" asked Vivian.

Eyes darting, Melanie twisted the ends of the shawl around her fingers. "No, not directly, but Besi was afraid of him."

"Do you know if Besi ever met with the guy?"

"She met with him in March," said Melanie. "She only agreed to the meeting because she thought the guy was a bookie who wanted money for a gambling debt that Derek couldn't pay, which upset her because Derek had promised to stop gambling. She was scared that Derek was in trouble again."

"Again?" asked Vivian.

Melanie rolled her eyes. "Besi was always bailing Derek out of jams. I didn't think she should meet with the guy. I wanted her to let Skip handle it."

"Skip?" asked Vivian, finding the name familiar.

"Skip Taylor," said Melanie. "Derek's fixer."

Nodding, Vivian remembered Leo telling her about the conversation he'd overheard between Derek and Skip Taylor.

"The two of them, Besi and Skip, were working together to make sure Derek stopped gambling so much and stayed out of trouble," said Melanie. "Anyway, Besi met with the guy, and when she returned, she seemed distracted, but she didn't talk about it much, just said she was going to deal with it."

"It just occurred to me," said Vivian. "If you have Besi's phone, then you can show those threatening emails to the police. They can trace the guy's IP address and find out who he is and where he lives."

"I wish I could, but when I was checking the current messages and texts on her phone," said Melanie, "I couldn't find the threatening emails. Besi might have deleted them."

"Do you know if she told Derek about the messages?" asked Vivian, thinking that Leo could question his old prep school nemesis.

"I'm not sure," said Melanie. "But, they might be on the other phone I found in Besi's things."

"What other phone?" Vivian asked. "Did Besi have two phones?"

"Not that I knew of," said Melanie. "But, the other phone was in her suitcase, so I assumed it was hers, but now I'm not so sure."

"Why not?"

Wrapping the shawl around her shoulders, Melanie said, "Because the new password didn't work on the phone I found in her suitcase. Besi had me change the password to something weird. Anyway, when I tried the new password, it didn't work, so maybe the other phone doesn't belong to Besi."

Vivian asked, "What was weird about the new password?"

Melanie stared at her for a moment and then shrugged. "Guess it doesn't matter if you know the new password. It's Guillermo Davis. Besi's old passwords were complicated, letters and numbers and symbols, upper and lower case. And she had a different password for every device she owned and for all of her accounts at various banks and stores. But, she wanted all the passwords changed to that name—Guillermo Davis."

"Did she tell you why?"

"I had a feeling that name meant something to her," said Melanie. "Maybe Guillermo Davis was someone she knew, but when I asked her, she just said it was a name she made up, and she figured no one would ever guess that it was her password."

Considering Melanie's theory about Besi's new password, Vivian removed her phone from the pocket of her denim blazer and entered the name Guillermo Davis in her note taking app.

"Anyway, I'll give you both of the phones," said Melanie. "Maybe the cops can find something to help them find Besi's killer."

"Hopefully," agreed Vivian standing.

Melanie looked up at her, and said, "I didn't tell the cops this, but … "

"But?" prompted Vivian, taking a seat again.

"Sometimes, I wonder if Besi was killed because of Derek." Glancing toward the wall of French doors, Melanie said, "Because of his gambling problem. I wonder if the guy who was harassing Besi killed her because she wouldn't pay any more of Derek's debts."

"I suppose that's possible," said Vivian.

Melanie looked at her again. "And then I think that Besi was killed by accident. What if the people Derek owed money to sent someone to kill him?"

Vivian frowned. "You think Derek was the target?"

Nodding, her green eyes shining with tears, Melanie said, "But, the killer missed that low life son of a bitch Derek and killed Besi instead."

11

"You got more information than I did," said Leo, walking to the bed where his wife sat with her legs crossed, staring at the screen of a cell phone. "Maybe you are the world's best investigative reporter."

Earlier at dinner—Lemmie's famous goat stew eaten in the breakfast nook in the kitchen, just the two of them—they'd discussed the progress of their informal investigation into Besi's murder. Leo didn't have much to report, but Vivian had gotten an earful from Melanie.

"You have to stop doubting me," said Vivian, giving him a sly smile.

Leo crawled onto the bed and positioned himself behind his wife. "Zeke and Jacob have no idea who would have wanted Besi dead."

"What did Tom say?"

"He thinks Winnie did it, but in some sort of twisted logic, he blames Derek for Winnie's actions," said Leo.

"Tom is heartbroken and grieving," said Vivian.

"I'm starting to wonder if Melanie might be right," said Leo. "Maybe some bookie did send a hitman to kill Derek."

"You did overhear Derek and Skip talking about someone who wanted a lot of money from Derek," reminded Vivian. "Maybe they were discussing a gambling debt."

"I don't think so. Derek didn't seem to know the guy which was why Skip said he had to find out more about him," said Leo.

Nodding, Vivian said, "If the guy was a bookie, then Derek would know him. So if the guy isn't a bookie, then who is he and why does he want money from Derek?"

"Who the hell knows?" Leaning forward to rest his chin on Vivian's shoulder, which gave him a view of the cell phone's screen, Leo asked, "You find anything interesting on that phone?"

"Actually, I did," said Vivian.

"Is that Besi's real phone?" asked Leo. "Or, the mystery phone Melanie found in Besi's luggage?"

"It's her real phone," said Vivian. "The new password doesn't work on the mystery phone."

"So whatever is on the mystery phone," said Leo, "remains a mystery."

"I think I know how we can unlock the mysteries on the mystery phone," said Vivian. "But, first—"

"Hey, you think if I say mystery one more time, we can take a shot?"

"Don't be silly," said Vivian. "Anyway, you asked if I'd found something interesting. Well, Besi got a text message last Wednesday from Skip Taylor, which said, 'We need to meet. Call me'. And then, in Besi's call log, I saw where she did call Skip."

"Maybe they met somewhere," said Leo.

Vivian asked, "Wonder what Skip wanted to talk to her about?"

"Probably fixing Derek's problem. But, wait, Skip sent Besi the text on Wednesday?" asked Leo, a memory sparking in his mind. "That is interesting because the day before, on Tuesday, is when I caught Derek and Skip talking about Derek's problem. Skip claimed he was leaving the island that day."

"Obviously, he didn't if he and Besi met on Wednesday," said Vivian. "And you know what else is interesting?"

"That we keep using the word interesting?" joked Leo, planting a kiss on Vivian's neck.

"Would you prefer curious?" suggested Vivian.

Leo considered the word. "I'm okay with curious."

"What's curious is last Wednesday is also the same day Besi faked a headache and took the BMW to go shopping," said Vivian. "I'll bet she went to meet Skip to discuss Derek's problem."

"I'll bet you're right."

"How much?" asked Vivian.

"What?"

"How much will you bet me?"

Flummoxed by her question, Leo stammered, staring at his sexy wife as she put Besi's phone in the drawer of the bed table and then returned to her position next to him.

"While you're thinking of a suitable wager," said Vivian. "I want to ask you—"

"Aren't you going to give Besi's phones to the police?" asked Leo.

"I'm going to give them to Stevie," said Vivian. "Maybe his hacker cousin can find the strange emails on Besi's phone and figure out the password on the mystery burner phone and find something useful."

Shrugging, Leo said, "As you were saying..."

"As I was saying what?"

"You wanted to ask me something?"

"Oh, that's right," said Vivian. "Do you know someone named Guillermo Davis?"

"Guillermo Davis?" Leo thought about the name.

"Does that name sound familiar?" asked Vivian. "Maybe he went to school with you, Derek, and Besi."

Leo shook his head. "Never heard the name before but that doesn't mean he didn't go to school with us? Why do you ask?"

"That's the new password Besi wanted to use after she was robbed in the Aerie Islands," said Vivian. "Besi told Melanie the name meant nothing to her, but I'm not sure about that."

Leo said, "Maybe you can have Sophie check it out. See if there's some connection between Besi and Guillermo Davis."

"Good idea," said Vivian.

As Leo slipped an arm around her shoulders, Vivian angled her body toward him, curling herself in his embrace.

"So, to recap," began Leo. "Besi gets a text from Skip Taylor about something important they need to talk about. He wants her to meet him.

You remember a few days before the wedding when Isaac told us Besi had borrowed the white BMW."

"Refresh my memory," requested his wife.

Leo said, "That was the day when we pulled into the garage and saw Isaac inspecting a busted tail light on the silver Mercedes."

Vivian frowned. "Busted taillight. Silver Mercedes."

"And remember we asked Lemmie who borrowed the Mercedes, and he told us Derek had taken it out for a midnight drive," said Leo. "When I asked Derek about it, he claimed he needed to clear his head."

Nodding, Vivian said, "Now I remember that day. Isaac said Besi had gone shopping, but maybe that wasn't true. Maybe she borrowed the car to meet Skip Taylor."

"Right. We need to find out where she and Taylor met," said Leo, pressing his lips against his wife's brow as she closed her eyes.

"If Skip gave her an address, how would she know how to find it?" asked Vivian, opening her eyes and tilting her head back to stare at him.

"All of Dad's cars have GPS."

"Maybe there's an address in the GPS log of the BMW," said Vivian. "We can check the log for the day Besi used the BMW and see if there's an address."

"Might be the address where Besi went to meet Skip Taylor," said Leo.

"It's worth a shot," said Vivian. "I'll talk to Isaac."

12

"How are you holding up?" Leo asked as he stood in the doorway of the second-floor den, staring at Derek, who slouched in one of the dark leather club chairs in the far corner of the room.

For the past few days, Leo had been hesitant about approaching Derek to ask him about Besi's murder. He wasn't quite sure how to start the inquisition, but he supposed there was no decent way to bring up the subject.

"How the hell do you think?" Derek took a sip of the dark amber liquid in his glass and grimaced. "My fiancée was shot to death right in front of me. So, I guess the answer to your question is, I'm not holding up."

Leo didn't know how to respond.

Most people professed to understand the grief of the grieving person, but Leo thought it would be disingenuous. He had no idea how Derek felt, nor did he want to, if he was honest. Leo didn't even want to think about losing Vivian to some heinous act of senseless violence. When he thought about his wedding day, Leo couldn't imagine what he would have done if Vivian had been shot as they were exchanging vows.

"Listen," Leo cleared his throat. "You have any idea who could have shot Besi?"

"I already talked to the cops, okay?" Derek took another drink and then swiped the back of his hand across his mouth. "I told them Besi didn't have an enemy in the world. She was the sweetest girl. She was a friend to everyone who knew her. But now that Winnie has confessed it makes perfect sense. Winnie has always hated Besi and been jealous of Besi. I'm not surprised that Winnie killed Besi. She's crazy enough to kill."

Shifting in his chair, Leo said, "Dad doesn't think Winnie killed Besi and I find it hard to believe myself."

"Winnie confessed," said Derek, his eyes glassy, darkening with drunken rage. "She killed Besi. The bitch needs to rot in jail for what she did."

"I know Winnie said she killed Besi," said Leo, trying to be sensitive and tactful, and not piss Derek off. "But, I don't think the evidence is going to prove her claims."

"Evidence? What the fuck?" Derek slammed the glass down on the small coffee table between the club chairs. "The cops don't need evidence. They have Winnie's confession. That's all they need to make sure she stays in jail for the rest of her fucking life!"

"Derek, to make a case that Winnie killed Besi," Leo started. "The cops need motive, means, and opportunity."

"Yeah, and Winnie had all three," said Derek, after another swig of his drink. "Motive—she hated Besi. Means—she could have easily bought a gun. Opportunity—she didn't leave the island even though she had no reason to stay here because she wasn't going to be in the wedding. Don't you wonder why? She stuck around so she could blow Besi's head off."

Shifting in his chair, Leo said, "It is weird that Winnie didn't leave St. Killian after she was kicked out of the wedding, but did she really hate Besi?"

"What is your problem?" Derek glared at him. "You want Winnie to get away with murder?"

"I want the person who killed Besi to be brought to justice," said Leo. "But, I don't think that person is Winnie."

"Then who do you think killed Besi?" Derek asked.

"That's what Dad wants me to find out," said Leo.

"What the hell do you need to find out?" Derek slammed the empty glass down on the coffee table. "The cops have the killer. Winnie confessed. And I know Burt probably doesn't believe that, but it's true. Winnie killed Besi."

"Why did Winnie hate Besi?" asked Leo, folding his arms as he leaned back in the club chair. "I haven't been in touch with you guys for some time, but I remember Winnie and Besi being friends. So, what happened?"

"How the hell do I know?" Derek shrugged and looked away. "Winnie's crazy. Who the hell knows why that psycho feels the way she does about anything."

"You said that Winnie was jealous of Besi," Leo said. "I can't imagine why. Alfred Quasebarth, the last time I checked, is worth about twenty billion, which is more than Samuel Beaumont is worth, although three billion is nothing to sneeze at."

"Neither is thirty-two billion," said Derek, smirking. "Last time I checked, that's how much your mom is worth."

"Second richest woman in France," said Leo, deciding not to let Derek's smarmy sarcasm bother him. "But, my point was money can't be the reason for Winnie's jealousy. So, maybe Winnie was jealous of Besi because you chose Besi instead of her?"

Sneering, Derek asked, "What the hell are you talking about? I didn't choose Besi over Winnie. I was never involved with Winnie."

"But, you could have been," said Leo. "Tom said you had a choice between Besi and Winnie. You chose Besi and—"

"Tom is a lying sonofabitch," said Derek.

"So, it's not true that you were only marrying Besi because you need money?" asked Leo, knowing that he was pushing his luck.

Shaking his head, Derek said. "How the hell can you ask me that? You believe Tom's bullshit? I loved Besi. That's why I asked her to marry me. She was supposed to be my wife. We were supposed to be on our honeymoon right now."

Feeling like shit, Leo rubbed his eyes. "Derek, I'm sorry, okay. I didn't mean to—"

"What did you mean to do, Leo?" Derek sneered. "Come in here and kick me when I'm down?"

Leo exhaled and then cleared his throat. "I'm just trying to find out who really killed Besi and why—"

"You know who killed Besi," said Derek, eyes flashing with anger.

"Listen, I don't want to upset you—"

"Then don't," warned Derek.

"I have to ask you about your gambling."

Derek's eyes narrowed to thin slits as his jaw clenched. "I don't gamble anymore."

"Melanie said you had some problems paying your gambling debts," said Leo. "And Besi bailed you out."

"Melanie is a busybody bitch who doesn't know what she's talking about," Derek said.

"Could Besi have been killed because of a debt you didn't pay?" Leo asked, deciding to put the question out there and let the cards fall where they may. "Could someone have shot Besi to send you a message?"

"How the hell could you ask me something like that?" Derek shook his head.

Doubtful that Derek would give him a straight answer, Leo said, "Well, let me ask you this: Why did you leave Hennessy Capital? Was it because of your gambling?"

"Who told you that?"

Leo said, "Tom said—"

Derek cut him off. "That jealous pussy doesn't know a damn thing about me."

"Why did you stop working for your dad?"

"Unlike you," said Derek. "I'm not going to let my father order me around and orchestrate my career path."

Leo felt a jolt of unease. "Burt doesn't order me around."

"Then why are you still working at the *Palmchat Gazette*?" asked Derek.

Glaring at Derek, Leo fought the urge to slug him.

"Your dad is better now," said Derek.

"Somewhat, but not quite," disputed Leo. "He's still got a ways to go before he's fully recovered."

"And what are you going to do when he does get back on his feet?" asked Derek. "Are you going to hang out in paradise wasting your talent? Or, are you going back to the Sudan where you belong?"

13

"What happened when you talked to Derek?" asked Vivian, joining Leo on the bed in their guest room on the second floor.

After a long, tedious day at the *Palmchat Gazette*, Vivian drove back to Burt's mansion where she was greeted by Lemmie, who informed her that dinner had already begun. She was expected to join Leo, Burt, and the wedding party, including Kelsea, who'd been informed that the St. Killian police wanted all members of the doomed ceremony to remain on the island until Besi's murder was solved.

Dinner had been a glum affair, grim and morose with awkward small talk. Lots of mumbled replies, furtive glances, and prolonged silences. Everyone doing their best to avoid the elephant in the room—Besi's murder and Winnie's arrest. Everyone terrified that someone would make the mistake of accidentally bringing up that heinous day.

Not even the chef's succulent roasted goat could save the meal.

As soon as the dessert course was finished, everyone hurried off to other places, scurrying away, anxious to escape each other and the horrific incident that would forever bind them, the day no one wanted to talk about, the day none of them would ever be able to forget.

"Don't ask," said Leo, dragging a hand down his jaw. "I brought up what

Tom said about him marrying Besi for her money. You can imagine how that went over."

Vivian made a face. "Did he slug you?"

"Surprisingly, no," said Leo. "Even though I probably deserved it."

"That explains why he was scowling at you during dinner," said Vivian, tucking her legs beneath her. "Did he have any idea who might have killed Besi?"

"As far as Derek is concerned," said Leo, "Winnie confessed so she must have done it. The conversation was a total waste of time. I asked him about his gambling and his reasons for leaving Hennessy Capital and got nothing except typical defensive posturing and deflection."

"Deflection?" questioned Vivian.

Leo exhaled. "He tried to shift the conversation away from himself by giving me crap about being forced to work for Burt. He was hoping to piss me off so I would stop questioning him."

"Did he piss you off?" asked Vivian, detecting an edge of resentment in her husband's tone.

"I knew what he was trying to do," said Leo. "And it didn't work."

Slightly hesitant, Vivian asked, "Are you sure that what Derek said didn't bother you?"

Leo glanced at her. "Why would it bother me?"

"Because maybe it's true," said Vivian. "Maybe you do feel forced to work for Burt."

"Even though it wasn't my idea to leave Africa," said Leo, "I don't regret my decision. My dad needed me and, honestly, when I found out you were in St. Killian, that sealed the deal."

Vivian smiled as Leo kissed her, but she wondered if her husband was being honest with himself about his feelings.

"Anyway, it's not like we're staying in St. Killian forever," said Leo, leaning back on the pillows propped against the tufted headboard. "As soon as Dad makes a full recovery, we can go back to the Sudan and pick up where we left off."

Vivian nodded, but her gesture of agreement felt disingenuous and deceptive. She didn't want to go back to Africa and pick up where they'd left off, which was heartbroken and separated. At odds over the future of their relationship. Divided by their opinions. Now that they were together, Vivian couldn't imagine why Leo wanted to go back to the place where they'd been torn apart.

"Did you get a chance to talk to Isaac about the GPS log in the BMW that Besi borrowed?" asked Leo.

Refocusing her thoughts, Vivian said, "There was an address in the GPS log of the BMW on the day Besi borrowed the car. It was the only address in the log. A house in Oyster Farms. On Dove Street. It's a vacation property."

Leo asked, "Is Skip Taylor renting that house?"

"I contacted the real estate company that manages the rental, but of course, they refused to tell me who's renting the place," Vivian said. "So, I did a drive-by. There was a Toyota in the driveway. I knocked on the door, but no one answered."

Stroking his jaw, Leo said, "I'll bet Skip Taylor was staring at you through the peephole and decided not to answer the door."

Vivian said, "We might have to do a stakeout. Catch him leaving the house and Shanghai him."

"Like we did to that defense minister in Mali who kept dodging us," said Leo, chuckling. "You stepped in front of him, and when he turned to run, I was behind him. Bastard was cornered. Had nowhere to go."

Anxious to move away from memories of their African exploits, Vivian said, "Anyway, in other news, Stevie's cousin hacked Besi's mystery phone. It's a burner, so he couldn't find out who it belongs to, but he recovered some deleted text messages that were very interesting."

"There's that word again," said Leo. "Interesting."

"Trust me," said Vivian, crawling over Leo to retrieve her phone from the bed table drawer. After returning to her spot, she accessed the file where she'd stored the information, and she said, "Someone texted: *We need to meet tonight. Urgent. Elizabeth can't be trusted. She won't keep quiet about what she knows.*"

"Who sent that text?" asked Leo. "And who did they send the text to?"

"The owner of the mystery burner phone sent the text to Besi," said Vivian.

Leo frowned. "Wait. So, Besi could've sent herself a text?"

Vivian shook her head. "I don't think the mystery burner phone was Besi's."

"I thought Melanie found the mystery burner in Besi's suitcase."

"She did, but she also said she didn't recognize the phone as belonging to Besi," Vivian reminded him. "I think that's because the mystery burner wasn't Besi's."

"Then how did Besi get the mystery burner?" asked Leo. "And who does it belong to?"

"Not sure," answered Vivian.

"Any leads on who Elizabeth is?"

"I thought you would know," said Vivian. "Maybe Elizabeth is a friend of Besi's? Or Derek's? Did you guys go to school with an Elizabeth?"

"Yeah, I'm sure we did, but I don't remember Besi or Derek having any close friends named Elizabeth," said Leo. "But, I don't know all of their friends."

"What I'm wondering is why Elizabeth can't be trusted?" asked Vivian.

"And what does she know that she won't keep quiet about?"

"Maybe something to do with Derek's gambling," suggested Vivian.

Leo said, "That's possible. Did Besi text the owner of the mystery burner back?"

Vivian stared at her screen. "Besi texted: *Fine. I'm at the house.*"

Leo said, "So, Besi met with the owner of the mystery burner."

"Apparently," said Vivian. "Then, a few hours later, Besi sends a text to the owner of the mystery burner, which reads: *It's Besi. Need to see you now! We have a problem!* And the owner of the mystery burner texted: *I'm on my way.*"

"You're right," said Leo. "That is interesting."

"Weird thing is that these texts were sent on the same day," said Vivian.

"Weird thing is not knowing the name of the owner of the mystery burner," said Leo. "And having to call that person, the owner of the mystery burner."

Vivian laughed. "Well, the last four digits of the mystery burner are 8977. How about that?"

"Guess that's okay," said Leo. "Okay, so, maybe 8977 didn't show up. Or, maybe 8977 showed up and left, and then something happened, and Besi needed 8977 to come back to the house."

"Because there was a problem," said Vivian. "But, what kind of problem?"

"An urgent one," said Leo. "Maybe involving Elizabeth? The woman who wouldn't keep quiet about what she knows. When were these texts sent?"

"In April," said Vivian. "When Besi was in the Aerie Islands getting her bump removed."

"You think these texts have anything to do with Besi's murder?" asked Leo. "I guess maybe Besi and 8977 were texting about Derek's gambling, but the texts aren't threatening to Besi."

"You're right," conceded Vivian as she powered off her phone. "And we're reading these texts completely out of context, so we can't draw any conclusions at this point."

Leo asked, "And what about the nasty emails Melanie said some guy sent to Besi's real phone?"

"Stevie's hacker cousin is still working on retrieving those," said Vivian.

Leo said, "Well, let's hope he finds the emails, and then we can tell the cops and let them handle the investigation, which is their job. Our job, despite what my father thinks, is to report on the results of the investigation."

"Guess we'll have to hold off on the speculation," said Vivian, returning her phone to the bed table. "We found out some interesting things, but we still don't have enough information to start forming any definitive conclusions."

"Well, gosh darn, Mrs. Bronson. Whatever shall we do now?" asked Leo, pulling her into his arms.

Vivian giggled as she wrapped her arms around his neck. "Well, Mr. Bronson, since we can't speculate, how about we fornicate."

14

"That was Sophie." Vivian tapped her phone to end the call with the junior reporter. "You're not going to believe this."

"What?" Leo grabbed a mango scone from the serving platter in the center of the breakfast table.

"The cops have the murder weapon that was used to kill Besi," said Vivian. "An AR-15 rifle. A maid at the Flamingo Inn motel in Little Turkey found it wedged in the coils of the springs under the bed when she was cleaning one of the rooms. She called the owner, and the owner called the cops."

"Flamingo Inn in Little Turkey," said Leo, taking a bite of the scone. "Why does that sound familiar?"

"Remember that story Sophie did about the guy found dead in Little Turkey?" asked Vivian. "Guy's name was Aaron Jones."

Chewing his scone, Leo nodded. "Cops found a Hermes briefcase and a hundred thousand dollars in a duffle bag in his motel room."

Vivian paused to take a sip of coffee before she said, "The gun used to kill Besi was found in the same motel room where Aaron Jones was found."

Dropping his scone, Leo stared at her. "Wait. What?"

"Jones was the last person to stay in that room," said Vivian. "The maid was cleaning the room because the owner planned to start renting the room again."

"Do the cops like Jones for the killer?" asked Leo.

"The police didn't mention anything about Aaron Jones renting the motel room," said Vivian. "Sophie made the connection. When she found out that the murder weapon was found in the same motel where Aaron Jones was found dead, she reviewed her notes and discovered that Jones was the last person to rent the room where the maid discovered the AR-15."

"When Jones was found dead," started Leo, "the cops collected evidence from that motel room, right? How did they miss the assault rifle?"

Shrugging, Vivian said, "Maybe they didn't think they needed to check under the bed?"

"Who is Aaron Jones, anyway?" asked Leo.

"Not sure," said Vivian. "He arrived in St. Killian about two weeks ago, but the cops don't know if he came to tour the island, or—"

"To kill Besi Beaumont," said Leo, exhaling.

Vivian said, "Just because the gun that killed Besi was found in Jones' motel room doesn't mean he shot her."

"The cops are sure the AR-15 they found is the gun that killed Besi?"

Vivian put an elbow on the table. "Ballistics confirmed it."

"What else did Sophie find out?" asked Leo.

"Nothing else from the cops, not yet anyway," said Vivian. "But she did give me an update on Guillermo Davis."

Leo frowned. "Who's that?"

"Remember I told you Guillermo Davis was the new password Besi used after she told Melanie to change all her old passwords?"

Nodding, Leo said, "Who is he?"

"Sophie found out that Guillermo Davis was from Bessemer, Alabama, which piqued her interest because Besi's real name is Bessemer. She kept digging and learned that Guillermo Davis once worked at the Beaumont estate in Bessemer, Alabama as Samuel Beaumont's driver. Sophie got in contact with a long-time member of the Beaumont staff who mentioned a rumor about Guillermo Davis having an affair with Besi's mom, Adrienne, which might be why Guillermo was fired."

"Now we know why Besi chose Guillermo Davis as her new password."

"Maybe. Maybe not," said Vivian. "Guillermo was fired a year before Besi was born. So, how would Besi even know him?"

"Maybe Besi grew up hearing the rumors about Guillermo and her mother?" Leo shrugged.

"Maybe," said Vivian, reaching for her glass of freshly-squeezed papaya juice. "Anyway, Sophie mentioned that Baxter François is holding another press conference tomorrow, so maybe we'll find out more details about the case."

Leo scoffed. "François isn't going to give up any details that might shed light on the situation. All you'll get from the detective is evasive maneuvering and vague deduction."

"Maybe Sophie should talk to Detective Janvier?" suggested Vivian.

Snorting, Leo shook his head. "Inspector Clouseau? He's even worse. You know what we should do, Mrs. B.?"

"What's that, Mr. B.?" asked Vivian.

"We need to find out more about Aaron Jones. Who is he? Did he know Besi? Did he come to the island to kill her? If anyone knows of a connection between Besi and Aaron Jones, it's probably either her assistant or her fiancée," said Leo.

"Good idea," said Vivian.

Leo smiled. "What else would you expect from the world's greatest investigative reporter?"

Giving her husband a quick kiss on the nose, Vivian teased, "Nothing less. After all, I always expect the best from myself."

15

At the knock on her door, Vivian glanced up from the dismal online traffic report she'd just downloaded and smiled at Detective Baxter François, who stood in the opened doorway of her office at the *Palmchat Gazette*.

"Detective François," said Vivian, tossing the report on top of a stack of files in the plastic IN BOX tray on her desk. "Come in. Have a seat."

After closing the door, the detective settled his muscled bulk into the chair in front of her desk.

"How are you?" asked Vivian, grabbing a red editing pen from the coffee mug she'd repurposed into a pencil and pen holder.

The detective exhaled. "I'll be a lot better when I figure out who killed Besi Beaumont."

"Why do you have to figure out who killed Besi Beaumont?" asked Vivian. "You arrested Winnie Quasebarth."

The detective gave her a sly smile. "Didn't you catch my press conference this morning on Sky news?"

"I sent Sophie to cover it," said Vivian, tapping the pen against her chin. "But I haven't gotten a chance to talk to her."

"Winnie Quasebarth didn't kill Besi," said François. "The charges against her have been officially dropped, which is what I shared with the press this morning."

Floored, Vivian shook her head. "How did you eliminate Winnie as a suspect?"

With an enigmatic smile, the detective said, "Winnie has an alibi. On the day of the wedding, when Besi Beaumont was being shot to death, Winnie was fooling around in her suite with two hotel pool boys."

"Two hotel pool boys?"

Detective François nodded. "When the pool boys read about Winnie's confession in the paper, they knew she was lying, but they didn't come forward because they were afraid of losing their jobs. Fraternizing with guests is cause for termination."

"So, how did you find out about Winnie and the pool boys?"

"One of the pool boys couldn't keep the hook-up to himself, and he told a friend about the threesome," said François. "That friend told another friend, who told another friend—"

"Who told another friend," said Vivian, not surprised that the pool boy had kissed and told.

"Eventually one of those friends told us," said the detective, "so we brought the pool boys in for questioning."

"And they spilled their guts all over the place under the pressure of those withering François interrogation techniques," said Vivian.

"Something like that," said François. "Anyway, one of the pool boys had some video of the encounter, which clearly showed Winnie Quasebarth dancing naked on a table. We determined that the video was recorded on the date and during the time when Besi Beaumont was killed."

"I guess that proves Winnie didn't kill Besi," said Vivian.

"I never considered her as a serious suspect, anyway," said François. "Especially after I got the tests back on the fabric left behind in the bushes and it wasn't a match for Winnie's bridesmaid dress."

Vivian stared at him. "What about the other bridesmaids' dresses?"

"You and the other bridesmaids are in the clear," said François. "Your dresses were analyzed, and all three dresses were found to be perfectly intact. No rips or tears in the fabric. There weren't even any loose threads."

"That's good to know," said Vivian.

"But, now I need another suspect," said the detective.

Tapping the pen against her desk, Vivian considered whether or not she should tell him about the threatening emails Besi had received six months ago. Confiding in the detective was the right thing to do, but Stevie's hacker cousin was still working on retrieving the deleted emails, so technically, she had no information to give him.

Deciding to forgo mentioning the threatening emails, Vivian asked, "What about Aaron Jones?"

"What about him?"

Realizing that the detective was going to play cat-and-mouse with her, Vivian tried to prepare herself for his customary evasiveness.

"Detective, how about we skip the part where you hold your cards close to the vest," suggested Vivian. "You and I both know that the weapon used in the murder of Besi Beaumont was an AR-15 found in a motel room in Little Turkey. And we know a tourist named Aaron Jones was found dead in that same motel room."

Smirking, the detective said nothing, just regarded her with an appraising gaze.

"Do you think Aaron Jones killed Besi Beaumont?"

"It doesn't matter what I think," said the detective. "The only thing that matters is the evidence."

"Does the evidence show that Aaron Jones killed Besi?" asked Vivian.

Detective François crossed his arms. "Off the record?"

Vivian said, "Only if you give the *Palmchat Gazette* an exclusive."

The *Palmchat Gazette* had suffered because of Burt's gag order concerning coverage of Besi's murder, but being the first news outlet to report on a major break in the case could send their online traffic numbers through the roof.

His expression wary, the detective asked, "What kind of exclusive?"

"When you figure out who killed Besi, and I have no doubt that you will," said Vivian, "then you'll tell me first and allow the *Palmchat Gazette* to break the story."

After a long exhale and more appraising looks, the detective said, "I'm waiting for a few more reports from forensics. We have prints on the gun, and I believe the evidence will show that Aaron Jones killed Besi Beaumont. Which, of course, is only half the story. The real question is why?"

"What about the money found in Jones' motel room?" asked Vivian. "What's the story with the cash? Is it connected to Besi's murder somehow?"

"I have not come to any definitive conclusions about the money."

Vivian suspected that the detective probably did have conclusions about the money, but he wasn't going to share them.

"What do you know about Jones?" Vivian asked.

Leaning forward slightly, François made a steeple of his fingers. "A lot of things don't add up with this guy. For instance, Jones checked into a cheap Little Turkey motel room, but he arrived on the island in style. Private plane. Flew in from the Aerie Islands two weeks ago."

"The Aerie Islands?" asked Vivian, thinking, for some reason, that she should make a note of that detail.

"I found out that Jones flew from Los Angeles, California to the Aerie Islands in April," said François. "CCTV shows him getting into a cab at the Amargo International Airport. I don't know where the cab took him, but his trip was more than just a weekend getaway or a two-week vacation."

"Jones was in the Aerie Islands from April to August," said Vivian. "Sounds like an extended stay in paradise to me."

"When I spoke to Melanie Adams, Ms. Beaumont's assistant," said the detective, "she informed me that Ms. Beaumont had traveled to the Aerie Islands a few months ago. In April."

Vivian nodded. "She went there for plastic surgery."

"Makes me wonder if there's a connection between Ms. Beaumont's trip to the Aerie Islands and Jones' trip to the Aerie Islands? Or, is it an odd coincidence?"

Vivian didn't believe in coincidences, but she wasn't sure how to make a connection between Aaron Jones and Besi. There weren't enough details, though the facts were strange. Jones and Besi both went to the Aerie Islands in April. And then, after arriving in St. Killian, they both ended up dead, shot to death. Bizarre circumstances, but Vivian didn't want to jump to conclusions just yet.

"If Jones and Ms. Beaumont did meet in the Aerie Islands," began François, "I'm thinking it was some kind of secret tryst."

Vivian said nothing as she recalled the secret hook-ups between Besi and Tom York. Was it possible that Besi and Jones had been undercover lovers, as well? Vivian doubted it, but she didn't think she should rule out any possibilities.

"You think Aaron Jones came to St. Killian to meet Besi?" asked Vivian.

"Suppose that's possible," said François. "But, then again, most men don't bring sand to the beach."

"What do you mean?" Vivian asked.

"Jones wasn't alone when he arrived in St. Killian," said François. "He was traveling with a dark-haired woman. Pilot says she never took off her sunglasses."

Vivian looked up from the Post-It note where she'd jotted down the information about Jones arriving in St. Killian from the Aerie Islands. "Sunglasses?"

The detective rubbed his chin. "Pilot thought it was weird. Says the brunette never spoke and kept her sunglasses on even though it was after midnight when they landed."

A brunette in sunglasses? Instantly, her mind conjured up the image of the woman she'd talked to at the cocktail party last week.

"The owner of the Flamingo Inn motel says he doesn't remember if Jones was with a brunette in sunglasses when he checked into the motel," said François. "However, he can't be sure of that fact because when Jones checked in, a large group of Europeans was checking in at the same time, and it was crazy busy. Plus, the owner and the hotel clerk were having issues with the new software they'd installed the week before."

"So, it's possible that Jones and the brunette did check into the motel together," said Vivian.

"The motel records don't reflect that," said Baxter. "When Jones checked in, he requested a room for one, but I think the brunette joined him."

"How can you be sure?" asked Vivian.

"We found dark hairs in Jones' motel room that did not belong to him," said François. "Tests showed that those hairs were not human but synthetic. Most likely from a dark brown wig—which might belong to the brunette."

"But, you don't know that for sure," Vivian pointed out.

"What I do know for sure is that the dark hairs found in the bushes at the crime scene don't match the dark brown hairs found in Jones' motel room.

The hair strands found at the crime scene were human, not from a synthetic wig. And the hairs at the crime scene were male."

"Are the hair strands found at the crime scene a match for Aaron Jones?" asked Vivian. "Did he have dark hair?"

Sighing, François rubbed his eyes. "Jones did have dark hair, but the initial tests were inconclusive, so we're sending the samples to another lab for more sophisticated analysis." "You have any idea who the brunette is?" asked Vivian, remembering the woman who'd said she was a friend of both the bride and the groom.

Standing, Detective François said, "I don't know her name, but I know why she came to St. Killian."

Slightly confused, Vivian shook her head. "What do you mean?"

The detective walked to the door, opened it, and then turned back to her. "She was here to help Aaron Jones murder Besi Beaumont."

16

"I can't believe those stupid island cops let Winnie get off," grumbled Derek as he stalked back and forth in front of the wall of bookshelves in Burt's home office. "That crazy bitch is getting away with murder!"

Slouching in one of the antique chairs in front of Burt's desk, Leo shook his head and then glanced at Vivian, sitting in the chair next to him. His wife looked a bit worried. Obviously, she found Derek's frantic pacing concerning, but Leo wasn't bothered by Derek's anxious agitation—or the reason behind it.

Following a late lunch with Burt and the wedding party, Leo and Vivian had planned to head back to the *Palmchat Gazette*, but his father had commandeered them. The St. Killian police department had new developments in the case, and Burt wanted Leo, Vivian, and Derek to be present when Detective Baxter François arrived.

While wasting time waiting for the detective, Leo told Vivian about his conversations with Melanie and Derek, where he'd asked them if Besi had known Aaron Jones. He'd planned to tell Vivian yesterday when she returned to the mansion following a long day at the newspaper, but the news about Winnie Quasebarth dominated their conversation. Winnie being officially cleared of murder charges was more interesting than the fact that both Melanie and Derek denied knowing anything about a connection between Jones and Besi.

Around three o'clock, Burt summoned them to his office in advance of Detective François' four o'clock arrival.

"The police cleared Winnie because she didn't kill Besi," said Burt, as imposing as ever behind his massive desk. "As I suspected, her confession was nothing more than a cry for attention."

"But, how can we know that for sure?" asked Derek. "Maybe Winnie planned this whole thing. She makes this confession that she knows no one will believe and then when no one believes her, she gets away with murder!"

Exhaling his irritation, Leo said, "Winnie didn't get away with murder. Not only was there no evidence to connect her to Besi's murder, but she had an airtight alibi. Winnie was boffing two pool boys in her suite at the Queen Palm when Besi was shot. You know that, Derek. Why you don't understand it, is beyond me."

"Okay, fine. Winnie didn't murder Besi." Huffed Derek, resuming his manic pacing. "Then who killed her? Do the cops even know?"

"We'll know soon, hopefully," said Burt. "As I said earlier, the police have developments in the case, and I invited Detective Baxter François to share them with us."

"Are you gonna tell the cops about those emails on Besi's phone?" Derek asked Leo. "Because they need to know, don't you think? Maybe whoever sent those threatening emails killed her?"

"What threatening emails on Besi's phone?" inquired Burt.

After Vivian explained that, according to Melanie, Besi had received threatening emails earlier that year, Leo said, "Viv and I are going to tell the police about the emails as soon as we hear from Stevie's hacker cousin."

Burt nodded. "Well, we'll refrain from sharing that information with the detective."

Fifteen minutes later, there was a knock on the door.

"Come in," said Burt.

The door opened, and Lemmie stepped inside the office to announce Detective Baxter François. Following greetings, François unbuttoned his beige linen sports jacket and took a seat in a third chair placed before Burt's desk.

"Mr. Hennessy," said François, staring at Derek, who'd stopped pacing and stood rooted to the spot in front of the bookshelves. "I'm glad you're here."

His expression wary, Derek asked, "Why?"

"Derek, why don't you pull up a chair," said Burt, though his tone made the suggestion sound more like a command.

After Derek complied with Burt's demand, François said, "I was hoping to talk to you."

Derek frowned. "I already talked to you. I gave you my statement, and I don't have anything else to say. I told you everything I know about Besi's murder, which is nothing at all."

Leo frowned. Why did Derek sound so shrill and manic? What was with all the fidgeting in his chair, as though he was unable to sit still?

"I have no idea who killed her," continued Derek. "I don't know who wanted her dead. That's what you're supposed to find out, but you haven't told me anything. So maybe you should tell me something. Tell me who killed Besi."

What was Derek so damn nervous about? Leo wondered. He seemed to be filibustering. Answering questions that no one had asked.

"I'll get to who killed Besi in a moment," said Detective François.

Interesting, thought Leo, glancing at Vivian. Her glance at him told Leo that she was just as intrigued by the detective's promise.

"First, I have some questions for you, Mr. Hennessy," said the detective.

"I'm not talking without my lawyer," insisted Derek.

Burt said, "Detective François, you mentioned new developments in the case? I'd like to hear about them if you don't mind."

Leo doubted that François appreciated Burt's subtle demands, but the detective cleared his throat, and said, "As you know, we found the murder weapon used to kill Ms. Beaumont."

"The AR-15 rifle," said Burt. "We are aware of that."

After a short exhale, François said, "You may also know that the gun was found in one of the rooms at a motel in Little Turkey, the Flamingo Inn."

"Can you please get to the stuff that we don't know?" demanded Derek.

"Derek, get ahold of yourself," ordered Burt. "Detective François, please continue."

The detective said, "Well, here's the stuff you don't know: The last person to occupy the motel room where the murder weapon was recovered was a man named Aaron Jones."

"What the hell does any of this have to do with who killed Besi?" Derek jumped up from his seat. "Who the hell cares about some guy in a motel room?"

As Burt demanded that Derek take his seat, Leo glanced at Vivian. As he'd expected, his wife seemed just as confused as he was about Derek's sudden irrational outburst.

"I told you that I would get to who killed Ms. Beaumont," said François, "and I am fairly certain that Aaron Jones killed Ms. Beaumont."

"Why are you only fairly certain?" asked Leo.

"Because these island cops don't know what the hell they are doing," said Derek, clutching the sides of the chair, knuckles white from his death grip. "You never should have been allowed to run this investigation!"

"Derek!" warned Burt, his tone suggesting he had lost all patience with his godson.

"We still need to confirm that the fingerprints found on the weapon belong to Aaron Jones," said François, unflappable, as though Derek's insults didn't faze him. "However, there is evidence that Ms. Beaumont was Jones' target."

"What's the evidence?" asked Vivian.

"We found a duffel bag in Jones' motel room," said François. "Inside were handwritten notes regarding a trip Ms. Beaumont made to the Aerie Islands in April. These notes included information about Ms. Beaumont's flight schedule. There was also an address written on an index card which turned out to be the location of Ms. Beaumont's estate in the Aerie Islands."

"How did this Jones person get Besi's travel itinerary?" asked Burt.

"I believe someone gave Jones the information," said the detective.

"Who?" asked Vivian.

"I'll get to that," said the detective. "But, first, you all are aware that Aaron Jones is dead, right? I think there was a story in the *Palmchat Gazette* about it. I was asked to provide a comment, but I declined."

"We know Jones is dead," said Leo.

"Who told Jones that Besi was headed to the Aerie Islands?" asked Vivian.

François said, "Ms. Beaumont didn't tell him. There's no evidence that she knew Aaron Jones. My theory is that Aaron Jones was hired to kill Ms. Beaumont. The person who hired Jones to kill Besi gave Jones her travel itinerary."

"Your stupid theory is bullshit!" Derek said, glaring at the detective. "No one would hire a hitman to kill Besi. That's ridiculous!"

François said, "We also found a Hermes briefcase in Jones' motel room which was—"

"We know that," said Leo, growing increasingly impatient with François' unnecessary plodding. "It was in the story we published in the *Palmchat Gazette*. There was a hundred thousand dollars in the briefcase."

"Leonard, please allow the detective to give us all of the details," said Burt.

The detective said, "I believe that money was Jones' payment for killing Ms. Beaumont. Now, the interesting thing is, we found Jones' fingerprints on the Hermes briefcase, which was not surprising, but there was also a second set of prints on the briefcase."

"Who did those second set of prints belong to?" asked Vivian.

"This is crazy!" Derek exploded. "If this Jones sonofabitch killed Besi, it was because he was obsessed with her, or something. No one hired the guy to kill her!"

"What makes you so sure of that?" Leo stared at Derek.

His eyes wild, Derek sputtered but seemed unable to manage a coherent sentence.

Burt said, "What about the second set of prints, detective?"

After a slight pause, Detective François said, "The second set of prints on the Hermes briefcase belong to Derek Hennessy."

17

A strange, suppressed silence smothered the room.

Leo glanced at Vivian, and then Burt, and finally at Derek. Disbelief covered their faces. Leo had the feeling that they were all struggling to absorb the shock of the bomb François had just dropped.

Had he heard the detective correctly?

"What the hell? That's not possible. That's crazy." Derek's tone was a high-pitched mix of outrage and confusion. "How the hell could my fingerprints be on some briefcase you found in a seedy motel room?"

"Detective François," began Burt, his expression concerned. "Can you please explain how you came to the conclusion that—"

"He can't explain because it's not true!" Derek shot to his feet.

François said, "When Mr. Hennessy was arrested for assaulting Mr. York, he was booked and fingerprinted. Those prints were compared to the second set of prints found on the metal clasp of the briefcase."

"What makes you think that briefcase belongs to me?" Derek asked.

"Do you have a Hermes briefcase?" asked Leo. Staring at Derek, Leo started to wonder if maybe the reason for Derek's agitation was guilt.

"Let's allow the detective to inform us," said Burt.

François said, "We found an item in the briefcase which strongly suggested that it belonged to Mr. Hennessy."

Derek scoffed. "That's impossible."

"It was your passport, Mr. Hennessy," said the detective. "We found it in an interior pocket of the briefcase."

"Someone must have stolen my briefcase," insisted Derek.

Leo remarked, "So, I guess that answers my question. You do have a Hermes briefcase."

"And I have to wonder, Mr. Hennessy," said the detective, "how your briefcase ended up in the motel room of Aaron Jones?"

"How the fuck should I know?" Derek thundered, resuming his frenzied pacing. "I told you. Somebody must have stolen it. There's no other way my briefcase could have ended up in that motel room. I certainly didn't take it there! Or, is that what you think?"

"I think that's exactly what you did," said Detective François.

Turning his withering glare on the detective, Derek asked, "Why the hell would I have given Aaron Jones a briefcase full of money? I don't even know Aaron Jones."

"You sure about that?" asked François.

"What is the point of these questions?" asked Derek. "You came here to tell us about some new developments with the case—"

"Which I did," said François.

"Yeah, some asshole named Aaron Jones killed Besi," said Derek. "But, he's dead, too, so he won't be brought to justice."

"You're right. Aaron Jones can't be arrested and put in jail," said the detective. "However, Ms. Beaumont will have justice."

"What does that mean?" Derek asked, lowering himself slowly back into the chair.

"Detective," said Burt, fixing his steely gaze on François. "I may be wrong, but I sense some insinuation in your tone. Do you have some accusation in addition to your revelation?"

Leo studied the detective as François gave Burt an evasive smile.

"I'd just like to ask Mr. Hennessy a few more things," said the detective, turning in his chair toward Derek. "Some details I'd like to clear up."

Exhaling, Derek asked, "What details?"

"Have you driven a silver Mercedes Maybach S560 while you've been on the island, Mr. Hennessy?" asked the detective, removing a cell phone from the inside pocket of his jacket.

Leo's pulse jumped.

"I have the license plate number information saved in my phone."

After François recited the plate number, Burt said, "I own that Mercedes, detective. It's one of the cars in my fleet. Why are you asking about it?"

"Was there some damage to it recently?" asked François.

Glancing at Vivian, Leo could tell that she, too, was remembering the broken taillight on the German sedan that Isaac had pointed out to them. Turned out, it was the car Derek had borrowed when he'd taken a midnight drive to clear his head.

Burt said, "I'm not sure. If there were, my garage manager, Isaac would have taken care of it."

"There was some damage to the car," Vivian spoke up and explained the situation with the taillight.

François said, "We found plastic chunks and shards on the ground outside of Aaron Jones' motel room. When forensics analyzed the shards, they determined that they were broken pieces from the taillight of a silver Mercedes Maybach. Mr. Hennessy, did you drive the Mercedes to the Flamingo Inn in Little Turkey?"

"Why the hell would I have done that?" Derek demanded. "I told you that I didn't know Aaron Jones."

Detective François sighed, and then said, "Mr. Hennessy, we found Jones' cell phone—that little detail was something I kept to myself so you wouldn't have read about it in the *Palmchat Gazette*—and we found several messages between you and Jones."

Shaking his head, Derek sputtered. "That's not possible."

"What do the messages say?" asked Vivian.

Leo was curious, as well, as his gaze drifted from Derek's panicked outrage to Burt's disappointment and skepticism as he regarded his godson.

"I don't have the transcripts in front of me," said François. "But, Mr. Hennessy and Aaron Jones were texting about money."

"Money?" asked Leo, sitting forward as he stared at the detective.

"That's a lie!" Derek said.

"Mr. Hennessy and Aaron Jones were discussing a payment that Mr. Hennessy was going to make to Aaron Jones," said François.

"That's bullshit!" Derek protested.

Burt said, "What kind of payment, detective?"

"Mr. Hennessy paid Aaron Jones to kill Ms. Beaumont," said the detective as he rose from the chair to stand. "And that's why, Derek Hennessy, you are under arrest for solicitation of the murder of Bessemer Elizabeth Beaumont."

18

"Dad just called," said Leo, closing the door behind him after he walked into Vivian's office at the *Palmchat Gazette*. "He bailed Derek out of jail, and they should be back in Montmarch in about an hour, or so."

"Did Burt say how Derek is holding up?" asked Vivian as she turned from her computer.

"I didn't ask," said Leo, dropping down onto the couch against the far wall directly opposite her desk. "And I don't care how he's doing. All I want Derek to tell me is the truth."

"You want to know if he hired Aaron Jones to kill Besi," said Vivian.

"I already know that Derek hired Jones to kill Besi," said Leo. "I want him to come clean and admit it. I don't want any more of his lies or half-truths or plausible denials."

"You've made up your mind, and you won't change it," said Vivian. "You believe Derek put a hit out on Besi."

"What else can I believe?" asked Leo, his tone incredulous as he stared at her.

"Derek said Jones was blackmailing him," said Vivian. "You don't think that's true?"

"For the record, no, I don't believe Jones was blackmailing Derek, but even if that is true, how did Besi end up dead?"

Vivian thought for a moment, struggling to come up with a plausible answer, something that made sense, a theory that wasn't based on unfounded conjecture.

Leo said, "The answer is, Besi doesn't end up dead if Jones was blackmailing Derek. If the hundred thousand dollars in the Hermes briefcase is a blackmail payment, then it means Derek complied with Jones' extortion demand. Jones has his money so why would he kill Besi? He wouldn't."

"Maybe Derek didn't comply with Jones' demands," suggested Vivian. "We don't have the texts between Derek and Jones. Maybe Jones wanted more than a hundred thousand. Maybe Jones asked for a million dollars, and when Derek gave him a tenth of that amount, maybe Jones killed Besi because Derek didn't hold up his end of the deal."

Leo shook his head. "Babe, you know that's not how blackmail works. If Jones wanted a million and Derek only gave him a hundred thousand, then Jones would escalate his threats to expose Derek. He wouldn't kill Derek's fiancée."

Frustrated, Vivian said, "I know, but—"

"Stop trying to come up with some alternative scenario. You heard the evidence against Derek," Leo said. "You were there when Baxter François laid everything out. It all makes sense."

"Does it, though?" asked Vivian, cautious as she considered how to raise her doubts and concerns about the allegations against Derek. "Are you sure that Derek wanted Besi dead?"

Leo gaped at her. "How can you think that he didn't? Vivian, the evidence against Derek is solid."

"I've been thinking about the evidence," said Vivian, reaching for an editing pen from the coffee mug she used to hold writing utensils. "I have some concerns."

"Are you serious?" Leo asked. "Are you saying you think Derek is innocent?"

"I didn't say I thought he was innocent," said Vivian. "I said I had concerns about the evidence against him."

Leo folded his arms. "What concerns?"

Vivian paused. She didn't want to cause an argument, though she was used to sparring with Leo when they had differences of opinion about stories they were investigating. Vivian wasn't one to back down or suppress her beliefs. She was never afraid to make a point or present her case, but she felt she would have to be careful when it came to Derek Hennessy.

Derek's alleged involvement in Besi's death was an issue that might become a point of contention and discord between them.

Vivian sighed, lifted her thick column of braided hair from her neck, and placed it over her left shoulder. "I just think it would be best to take a hard, critical look at the evidence Baxter presented and not jump to a definite conclusion."

"You think I'm jumping to conclusions? You think I haven't thought about the evidence? I haven't stopped thinking about it," said Leo. "I keep going over it and over it in my head, trying to come up with a different conclusion, one where it doesn't seem possible that Derek hired Jones to kill Besi, but I haven't been able to do that."

François' bombshell about the texts between Derek and Jones didn't sit well with Vivian. The detective hadn't allowed them to see the transcripts of the texts. He'd paraphrased the messages, claiming that Derek had paid Jones to kill Besi? But, was that true?

Leo would probably agree with her about the text messages if his bitterness didn't blind him toward Derek. Her husband could be willfully stubborn, at times. She knew he wasn't in the mood to entertain any scenario in which Derek wasn't guilty.

Vivian decided to keep her doubts about the evidence against Derek to herself. For now.

Running a hand down the back of his unruly waves, Leo said, "Just pisses me off that Derek could get away with having Besi killed just like he's gotten away with all the other rotten shit he's done."

Vivian stared at Leo.

She'd been worried about how Derek's arrest had affected her husband. After seeing his childhood frenemy led away in handcuffs, Leo had been sullen and sarcastic.

Leo's sulking concerned her. In the two days that had passed since Derek's arrest, Vivian had tried her best to cajole and coax Leo out of his bad mood, but he seemed content to wallow in misery and melancholy. Her husband had exhibited disappointed ire toward Derek, but Vivian suspected Leo was truly saddened by the gut-wrenching allegations against Derek. Leo had professed nothing but annoyance with Derek since his arrival in St. Killian. Nevertheless, Vivian had a feeling that Leo cared more about Derek than he wanted to admit, or maybe even realized.

"You ready to call it a day and head out to Montmarch?" asked Leo.

"Just let me answer a few more emails," said Vivian. "Then I'll be ready to go."

"I want to grab some files from my office," Leo said, standing. "I'll meet you in the lobby in ten."

After her husband left, Vivian turned back to her computer. Fingers flying over the keyboard, she tried to concentrate on her task, but couldn't help worrying about Leo. She hoped her husband's animosity toward Derek wouldn't cause him to ignore evidence and allow an innocent man to go to jail for something he didn't do.

19

Disappointed and disgusted, Leo stared at Derek.

His face haggard and sallow, Derek was unshaven and unkempt. His eyes, haunted and bleary, darted back and forth as he dropped down into the chair on Vivian's right. He was wearing the same clothes he'd been wearing when Baxter François arrested him. The custom-made dress shirt was wrinkled, as were the linen trousers.

Shifting in the antique chair in front of Burt's desk, trying to get comfortable, Leo was sickened by a horrible case of the worse de'ja vu he'd ever experienced. Everything that had occurred in his father's office two days ago flooded his mind, a deluge of memories that nearly drowned him.

Derek Hennessy, you are under arrest for solicitation of the murder of Bessemer Elizabeth Beaumont.

As soon as the detective said those words, chaos and unbelief and confusion took over. Derek went berserk, shouting obscenities and screaming his denial of the detective's claims. Burt was outraged, expressing his incredulity and questioning François' detective skills. Vivian tried to be the voice of reason, desperate in her suggestions that everyone remain calm and rational.

A measured and practical response had been impossible.

Eventually, Burt managed to convince him to settle down so François could read him his rights. Stone-faced and silent, Derek didn't put up a fight when François put him in handcuffs and escorted him out of Burt's office.

Even now, two days later, Leo struggled to process the situation. Part of him couldn't believe that Derek had been arrested, but the evidence François had presented against Derek was compelling and convincing.

Derek's fingerprints had been found on the Hermes briefcase the cops recovered from Aaron Jones' motel room. Derek's passport had been found in the briefcase. Derek and Aaron Jones had exchanged text messages about some sort of payment. Derek had driven to the Flamingo Inn, leaving behind plastic shards from the taillight on the Mercedes he'd damaged.

Leo could only come to one conclusion.

Derek was guilty as hell.

With a long, weary exhale, Burt sat behind his desk. The leather chair groaned beneath his weight as he put his elbows on the table.

"Derek, I know that you have been through hell and, after two nights in jail, I'm sure you just want to take a shower and get some rest," said Burt, "but before you do, I need you to answer a few questions."

"I don't need answers," said Leo, leaning forward to stare at Derek. "I need the truth. Did you hire Aaron Jones to kill Besi?"

Shaking his head, Derek said, "I can't believe you think—"

"Derek, you need to start explaining," demanded Burt. "What the hell is going on?"

Running a hand through his greasy hair, Derek said, "This whole nightmare started before the wedding. Out of the blue, I get an email from a guy – he tells me his name is Aaron Jones and claims he has information about me that, if it got out, would ruin my life."

"What did you do?" asked Leo.

"I called Skip," said Derek.

"Skip Taylor?" asked Burt.

Derek nodded.

Leo glanced at this father and asked, "You know Skip?"

Burt exhaled, rubbing his eyes. "Not personally. We've never met but I know of him, and the services he provides."

"What kind of services?" asked Vivian.

"Skip Taylor is a fixer," said Burt.

His suspicions confirmed, Leo glanced at Vivian, who raised an eyebrow in acknowledgment.

"Skip's father, Chip Taylor, served in that capacity for David Hennessy," said Burt.

"So how did Skip handle the situation?" asked Leo.

Derek sighed and rubbed his jaw. "Skip called the guy, found out what he wanted. Aaron Jones was blackmailing me."

"What did Jones have on you?" Vivian asked.

Rubbing his haggard face, Derek said, "I don't know what Jones had on me. Skip was taking care of it, so I didn't ask questions. Didn't want to know, to be honest."

"You didn't want to know?" Dumbstruck by Derek's willful ignorance, Leo shook his head.

"Skip said he would take care of it," said Derek, a spark of defensiveness in his tone. "Skip fixes things. I trust him to take care of problems, so I don't have to worry about them."

Vivian said, "Skip coordinated and facilitated the blackmail payment to Jones."

Derek nodded. "Skip said Jones would keep quiet and hand over the evidence he had on me for a hundred thousand dollars."

"How did you come up with a hundred thousand dollars?" Leo asked. "You don't have a job anymore."

"I have access to other funds," said Derek.

"Yeah, Besi's funds," said Leo. "That secret offshore account she set up for you in the Aerie Islands."

Derek looked confused. "What secret offshore account? I don't know—"

"Why am I not surprised that you don't know?" Leo shook his head. "And I'm guessing you don't know that Skip called Besi a few days before the wedding to meet with him to discuss something very important?"

Derek shook his head. "Skip didn't tell me about meeting with Besi. I told him not to ask her for money because I didn't want her bailing me out—"

"Again?" asked Leo.

Exhaling, Derek said, "Skip arranged for one hundred thousand dollars to be transferred from my bank account to the Pourciau Bank and then he arranged for the cash to be withdrawn. Skip gave me the money, and I put it in my Hermes briefcase. Then I left the house to meet Skip and Jones at Jones' motel."

"You borrowed the silver Mercedes," said Leo. "Drove to the Flamingo Inn."

"When I got to the motel, Skip was already there, and he came out, alone, and told me he would give Jones the money," Derek said. "So, I gave him the briefcase. Skip said it was best if I didn't meet Jones, and I was fine with that. Skip went back inside the motel room, and I left the motel."

"But, before you left," said Leo, "you damaged the taillight."

Derek gave them a sheepish half-smile. "I was so nervous; I shifted into reverse instead of drive—I had backed into the parking space—and hit a column. I didn't realize what I'd done, so when you asked me, Leo, I didn't lie."

The contrite sincerity in Derek's tone threatened to prick Leo's heart, but he stilled himself against wayward emotions.

"Then I came back to the house," said Derek. "In my mind, Skip was fixing things, so I didn't have to worry. Then Besi was killed, and that island cop accused me of hiring Jones to kill Besi, which is crazy."

"Doesn't seem so crazy to me," said Leo, risking another disapproving glare from his wife—which she promptly gave him.

"It's crazy because I didn't want Besi dead. I didn't hire anyone to kill her, especially not Jones. He's not a hitman. He's a sleazy blackmailer," insisted Derek.

Burt exhaled and fixed his gaze on his godson. "Even though you kept crucial information from me—"

"In other words, Derek, you lied like the lying liar you are," said Leo.

"Leo," said Vivian, scolding him before his father had the chance to.

Vivian's scowl bothered Leo. Obviously, his wife agreed with his father about giving Derek the benefit of the doubt. Leo wasn't sure why, but he wasn't surprised. Derek had always been able to elicit compassion and sympathy from people—especially when he didn't deserve it.

Right now, there was no reason to mollycoddle Derek. And yet, he was getting the kid glove treatment. Burt was being protective. Vivian was understanding.

Leo didn't care. He was determined to maintain a healthy dose of suspicion.

Still, Leo found himself inwardly cringing when he recalled the wounded expression in the wide-eyed look of surprise on Derek's face moments ago. Why was he questioning his harshness? Why was he silently berating himself for his cynicism?

Derek didn't deserve any sympathy or understanding. Leo didn't want to give Derek the benefit of the doubt. But, neither did he want to kick the guy while he was down.

"The situation does not look good for you, Derek," Burt said. "I believe your account of the night in question—"

"Why am I not surprised?" asked Leo.

"Leonard, please," said Burt, pointing a warning finger at him. "I have lost all tolerance for your sarcastic barbs."

Saying nothing, Leo slouched in his chair, feeling too damn much like he was sixteen years old again, being berated and reprimanded for bullshit Derek had done.

Burt said, "Derek, my belief in you may not matter. The case can be made, rather convincingly, that you hired this Jones fellow to kill Bessemer. The fact that your briefcase, filled with the payoff money, was found in Jones' motel room—"

"That wasn't supposed to happen," said Derek. "Skip was supposed to bring the briefcase back to me. I don't know why he let Jones keep it."

"It also doesn't look good that you went to Jones' motel room," added Vivian.

"But, I didn't go inside," said Derek. "You can ask Skip. I'll give you his number."

"Derek, I'd like Leonard to speak to Skip Taylor in person," said Burt. "Where is he staying?"

"Not sure." Derek frowned. "I didn't ask."

"Of course, you didn't," Leo couldn't help saying.

"I never do," said Derek. "Skip says it's best if I know as little as possible when it comes to the details so that I can have plausible deniability."

"You know why people need plausible deniability?" asked Leo, glaring at Derek. "Because they've done something illegal."

"It's not illegal to pay a blackmailer, is it?" asked Derek, his expression confused.

"What do you think Jones had on you?" asked Burt.

Derek averted his gaze, studying his hands. "Maybe he knows why I left Hennessy Capital. I messed up. That's why Dad won't have anything to do with me."

"How did you mess up?" asked Leo.

"If the truth came out," said Derek, shaking his head. "Everything will be ruined. My family and everything that dad has worked so hard to build. It'll all be shot to hell because of me and my stupid mistakes."

"What the hell did you do?" Leo demanded, his impatience increasing.

"I can't tell you, okay?" Derek sighed. "But, I regret what I did, and how I disappointed my father, more than you know. I hate myself, even more, knowing that I gave money to the bastard who killed my fiancée."

Leo scoffed. "You think I'm buying this grieving would-have-been widower routine? You think I believe Jones was blackmailing you? You gave money to the bastard who killed your fiancée at your request."

"That is not true!" Derek said, banging his clenched fists against the arms of the antique chair. "I did not want Besi dead. I loved Besi. I know you don't believe that Leo, but it's true! I wanted to live the rest of my life with Besi. I can't believe she's dead. And I don't understand why Jones killed her."

Jones killed Besi because you paid him to, thought Leo, but for some reason, he couldn't bring himself to say the words. Not because he didn't believe them. He believed Derek was guilty, but he didn't want to.

Leo wished he didn't believe that Derek was capable of hiring some lowlife thug to kill Besi.

"I've been thinking about this nightmare," said Derek. "Someone must be trying to set me up?"

"That's what you've come up with," said Leo, shaking his head. "You're being framed?"

"I don't think that's so impossible," said Vivian, glancing at Leo.

Leo gave his wife a look. "Are you serious?"

Sitting back in his chair, Burt stroked his chin. "Perhaps someone set things in motion to make it appear as though Derek was being blackmailed by Jones so that there would be proof of payment from Derek to Jones."

Vivian said, "Exactly. Remember, Baxter François said the texts between Derek and Jones mentioned a payment, but we didn't see transcripts of those texts. How do we know Derek and Jones were finalizing a payment for a contract on Besi's life?"

"We don't need transcripts," said Leo. "We can ask Derek. What did the texts say? What kind of payment were you talking about?"

Derek's face crumpled. "I don't know."

Leo gaped at him. "You don't know?"

Vivian said, "I don't understand."

"When Skip took over to fix stuff," said Derek, "he asked me to give him my phone. He said he wanted to trace the guy's number. I think that's how he found out who Jones was. Anyway, he sent some texts to Jones, from my phone, and I guess they were texting about money."

"But, you're not sure, are you?" asked Leo, growing increasingly annoyed by Derek's deceit.

"Skip deleted all the text messages from Jones," said Derek.

"That's convenient," said Leo.

"It's the truth," insisted Derek, a hitch in his voice. "I know you don't believe me, but—"

"You're right, I don't believe you," said Leo, glaring at Derek as he stood. "I've had enough of your lies. You haven't changed. You've only gotten worse. You're still the same lying, conniving sonofabitch—"

"Leo," warned Vivian, scowling at him.

Undeterred by his wife's admonishing, Leo said, "I know you hired Aaron Jones to kill Besi. And if Jones wasn't dead, he could prove it. But, that's convenient, too, for you. Jones isn't around to tell us how you solicited him to commit murder. And something tells me, that's just the way you planned it."

"The way I planned what?" asked Derek, eyes wide. "What are you talking about?" "First, you had Besi killed," said Leo, glaring at Derek. "Then you got rid of Aaron Jones."

20

"You don't believe that Derek had Aaron Jones killed, do you?" asked Vivian, closing the door behind her after she walked into Leo's office at the *Palmchat Gazette.*

Instead of looking up from his computer to greet her, Leo continued to stare at the screen as he tapped on the keyboard.

Vivian fought to tamp down the frustration rising within her.

She didn't want to henpeck her husband, but she felt he owed her an explanation concerning his conclusion that Derek had a hand in the murder of Aaron Jones. Vivian was beyond irritated with his attempts to avoid the subject.

Yesterday, after accusing Derek of having something to do with Aaron Jones' murder, Leo had stomped out of his father's office, leaving behind a strained silence filled with shock, confusion, and anger. After she'd managed to calm Derek and smooth Burt's ruffled feathers, Vivian returned to their guest room, but Leo wasn't there. Instead of searching the vast estate, Vivian had texted her husband. Leo replied that he was taking a walk on the beach and needed time alone to think. Vivian waited up, but when he walked into the guest room two hours later, he wasn't in the mood to talk about his harsh, damning accusations against Derek.

This morning, when Vivian woke up, Leo was already gone. On her phone, a text informed her of an early meeting with overseas investors. Her husband usually did everything he could to avoid Bronson Publishing business. His eagerness to meet with the investors was nothing more than a diversionary tactic, but Vivian was prepared to navigate Leo's avoidance maneuvers.

"That's exactly what I believe," said Leo, still focused on the computer screen.

"I want to know why," Vivian said, walking toward his desk. "Leo, you can't just hurl an accusation like a grenade and then turn your back on the damage that was done."

Scoffing, Leo said, "I didn't do nearly as much damage as Derek did."

Vivian exhaled, crossing her arms over her chest. "Explain to me why you think Derek had Aaron Jones killed."

"You're the world's greatest investigative reporter." Leo glanced at her. "Can't you figure it out?"

"Leonard," Vivian said, glaring at him. "I'm not in the mood, okay? I've been busy all day, I had to skip lunch, and right now, I should be in a meeting with the production department, but I canceled it because we need to talk about your accusations against Derek."

Shaking his head, Leo leaned back in his chair and stared at her. "You want to know why I think Derek had Jones killed?"

"I've been waiting since yesterday," Vivian snapped.

"Remember that duffle bag the cops found in Jones' hotel room?" Leo asked.

Nodding, Vivian said, "The bag contained information about Besi's travel plans. Someone gave Jones that information."

"Not someone," said Leo. "Derek."

Disturbed by his decision to believe the worse about Derek, Vivian shook her head.

"No, think about it," said Leo. "Besi was murdered on her wedding day, in St. Killian. So why would Jones have her Aerie Islands travel itinerary?"

Not quite sure where her husband was heading, Vivian waited for him to continue before she commented.

"I believe that Jones was supposed to kill Besi in the Aerie Islands," said

Leo. "But, for some reason, he didn't get the job done. So, he had to travel to St. Killian to murder her."

"You think Derek wanted Besi dead before they had a chance to walk down the aisle?" asked Vivian. "Why? You think he had cold feet? If that was the case, he could have pulled a runaway groom. He didn't have to kill her to get out of marrying her."

"I'm not sure why Derek wanted Besi dead," said Leo. "But, he did. So, he hired Jones. Or, rather, Skip hired Jones. And then Skip probably killed Jones, at Derek's request."

"Let me see if I have this straight," said Vivian. "Your theory is that Derek wanted Besi dead, so he gave his fixer, Skip Taylor, the task of finding a hitman to kill her. The hitman, Jones, was supposed to kill Besi while she was in the Aerie Islands getting plastic surgery, but that didn't work out, so Jones traveled to St. Killian to kill Besi."

"And then Derek told Skip to kill Jones," said Leo. "Most likely, Derek wanted to make sure that Jones would never be able to rat on him."

Tilting her head, considering her husband's theory, Vivian asked, "Let's say you're right. Why would Derek and Skip leave behind evidence in Jones' motel room that implicates Derek?"

"Red herring clues," said Leo. "Evidence designed to corroborate Derek's story about paying Jones money as part of a blackmail scheme. You know who we need to talk to? The woman who came to St. Killian with Jones. The brunette who wouldn't take off her sunglasses."

Vivian asked, "Why do we need to talk to her?"

"I agree with François' theory about her," said Leo. "She was working with Jones. We need to find the brunette. She'll prove that I'm right about Derek."

"What about finding Skip Taylor?"

Leo asked, "What do you think he's going to tell me? The truth?"

"Why do you assume he'll lie?" Vivian asked.

"Skip is a fixer, Viv," said Leo. "That's what fixers do. They lie. That's how they fix things. He's going to tell me exactly what Derek wants him to tell me."

"Skip can give us the details that Derek doesn't know," said Vivian. "For instance, what evidence did Jones have on Derek. Skip can tell us more about the text messages he exchanged with Jones. Skip can tell us what he and Besi talked about. I'm sure he wanted to discuss the payment to Jones."

"Talking to Skip Taylor would be a waste of time."

Vivian shook her head. "I disagree."

"I don't believe for one moment that Skip took over the situation with Jones so that Derek could keep his hands clean," said Leo. "Derek has blood all over his hands—Besi's blood."

21

Cursing under her breath, Vivian frowned as she stared at her computer.

She'd read the latest budget report from the accounting team twice already, and the numbers still didn't seem to make sense. She couldn't concentrate. She couldn't focus.

Vivian rubbed her temples, feeling the beginnings of a headache.

For the past three days, she'd been irritable and cranky. She might have blamed it on her period, but it wasn't her time of the month. Vivian knew the reason for her bad mood.

The reason crawled into bed next to her every night.

Leo was getting on her last nerve.

She was so over his bitterness and resentment against Derek. He was allowing those destructive feelings to cloud his judgment. In his zeal to convince himself of Derek's guilt, he willfully overlooked evidence that pointed to Derek's innocence.

There was no clear motive for Derek to want Besi dead, but Leo didn't think that mattered. The police still hadn't released the transcripts of the texts between Derek and Jones, despite repeated requests from the team of defense attorneys Burt had retained to represent his godson. It was entirely possible that the content of the texts had been misconstrued or misunderstood, but Leo didn't believe that.

Vivian turned from the glare of her computer screen and rubbed her eyes.

She didn't like being opposed to her husband on the issue of Derek's involvement in Besi's murder.

Leo had decided that Derek's participation in Besi's death was a foregone conclusion. Wasn't like her husband to be so resolute and unyielding in his opinions. He'd always been able to be objective. As journalists, they were both committed to fair and balanced reporting without any personal bias.

Why was her husband so obtuse and narrow-minded? Why was he refusing to consider that he might be wrong about Derek?

A knock on the door interrupted her thoughts, but Vivian was glad to focus on something else.

"Come on in," she called out.

Sophie Carter entered. Dressed in yellow Bermuda shorts with a matching jacket, she was all sunshine and happiness with her infectious grin and springy, natural curls bouncing in time with her jaunty walk.

Despite her best efforts not to, Vivian frowned.

Sophie's smile faded as she walked to the chair in front of Vivian's desk. "You okay? Were you in the middle of something? I can come back if—"

"No, no, it's just ..." Vivian stopped, struggling to come up with an excuse for her sour mood.

"What?" asked Sophie, concern in her soft brown eyes.

The sympathy in the junior reporter's gaze made Vivian long for a trusted confidant. With an acute forlornness, she was instantly reminded that the one person she'd been able to talk to about anything was lost to her forever—her best friend, Amal.

"Viv?" prompted Sophie

"Leo is acting like a stubborn jerk," Vivian blurted out, surprised at her admission.

Sophie's eyes widened.

"He refuses to believe that Derek is telling the truth," Vivian said and went on to list her grievances against her husband and his resolute belief in Derek's guilt.

"Can I ask you something?" asked Sophie.

"Okay ..." said Vivian, hoping she wouldn't regret her decision to confide in Sophie.

"Why are you so sure that Derek isn't guilty?"

"Because ..." Vivian trailed off, no longer sure that her belief in Derek's innocence was steadfast or unwavering. "There's no conclusive, definitive proof of his guilt. There's no evidence that he paid Aaron Jones to kill Besi. Detective Francois claims there are texts between Derek and Jones about some payment, but the police haven't released those texts. How do we know that Derek and Jones were texting about how much Derek was going to pay Jones to kill Besi?"

"How do you know that Derek and Jones weren't texting about killing Besi?" suggested Sophie.

"Derek said Jones was blackmailing him," said Vivian. "Jones contacted Derek to make an extortion demand."

Sophie asked, "But, how do you know that's true? Because Derek Hennessy said so? How well do you even know him? Didn't you just meet? And how long has Leo known Derek?"

"They grew up together," said Vivian.

Nodding, Sophie said, "I know you want Leo to look at the situation objectively, but maybe he can't. An unbiased perspective is probably impossible considering what Leo knows about Derek."

Vivian tapped her pen against her cheek. "I suppose you're right."

"Maybe you should think about the situation from Leo's point of view," suggested Sophie. "Maybe his reasons for thinking that Derek is guilty are just as valid as your reasons for thinking that Derek is innocent."

Reflecting on Sophie's perspective, Vivian felt convicted of her obtusiveness. Wasn't she somewhat guilty of the very offense she'd accused her husband of committing? Wasn't she single-minded in her belief that Derek was innocent of hiring Jones to kill Besi? She was upset with Leo for refusing to look at the evidence objectively, but her husband had examined the evidence. And he'd come to a different conclusion. A conclusion Vivian didn't agree with, but she had no right to assume that Leo only believed Derek was guilty because of a predisposed prejudice.

"Oh, Sophie, you're right," said Vivian, dropping her head in her hands. "I'm such a bad wife. This whole situation has probably been so much more difficult for Leo than I even realized. I need to be supportive and understanding. I need to apologize to my husband."

Sophie said, "And while you're apologizing, you could also tell him what I found out."

Vivian lifted her head from her hands to stare at Sophie. "What did you find out?"

Her eyes alive with excitement, Sophie said, "Officer Fields gave me some off the record information about the Besi Beaumont murder case."

"What did Fields tell you?"

"A maid at the Flamingo Motel remembers seeing a brunette woman in large sunglasses leaving Aaron Jones' motel room the day he was killed," said Sophie.

Vivian thought of the mysterious brunette she'd talked to at the engagement party and seen at the wedding, the woman Detective François believed was Jones' accomplice.

"And another motel employee, the late night desk clerk, now remembers that he checked the brunette into the motel," said Sophie. "Apparently, the night Jones checked into the Flamingo Inn, the motel was super busy."

Vivian nodded. "François told me that. There was also some issue with the motel's computer system."

Sophie said, "Right. Anyway, the night clerk remembers that the brunette in sunglasses requested her own room. The clerk gave her room fifteen. Jones had room nine. The clerk didn't think they were together. Both Jones and the brunette paid cash. The motel usually makes you show a photo ID to rent a room, but she paid for a two-week stay, so the clerk says the owner said it was okay to waive that requirement."

"Why am I not surprised?" Vivian asked.

Sophie nodded. "The brunette claimed she'd lost her license. However, she did give the clerk her name."

Vivian said, "So, the police have identified her … "

Removing her phone from her pocket, Sophie swiped the screen with her thumb. "I put her name in my notes … she is … Elizabeth A. Davis."

22

"Got a second?" asked Vivian, knocking on the door frame.

Glancing up, Leo nodded and beckoned for his wife, standing just outside the threshold into his office, to come inside.

As Vivian closed the door behind her, Leo tapped his phone, ending the call he'd been about to make—a call he wasn't exactly excited to make and which he didn't think would be successful, considering that his previous attempts had also failed.

Placing the phone on the mouse pad, he stared at Vivian, trying to gauge her mood.

His wife has been pissed at him for the past few days, since their last conversation, a contentious debate during which he'd declared his unwavering belief in Derek's guilt. Subsequently, their discussions about Derek and Besi's murder had been focused on how they would cover the story in the *Palmchat Gazette*. Dwindling numbers had convinced Burt that the paper couldn't afford to "catch and kill" the story. The *Palmchat Gazette* was in a unique position to take advantage of the exclusive information it was privy to.

Leo had been allowed to write first-person accounts from everyone in the wedding party, including Derek, though Burt and the lawyers advised against any direct quotes from Derek.

Vivian had scored an exclusive with Detective François. Her article, which reported that Aaron Jones was the main suspect in Besi's death, had driven online traffic into the stratosphere. The story had been picked up by news organizations all over the world. As a bonus, online subscriber rates increased, which helped ad rates rebound.

As happy as everyone was about the paper's recent accomplishments, Leo knew that he and Viv were allowing success to distract them from their differences of opinion about Derek.

The division was still between them, just below the surface, the elephant in the room they ignored and shunned. Unofficially, they'd decided not to talk about their conflict. The hidden strife manifested itself in other ways, however. They found creative ways to avoid accidentally bringing up the dreaded topic—Derek Hennessy. Worse thing was, their sex life was suffering. For the past few days, there'd been too much space between them in the massive king-sized bed.

Viv wanted him to be more objective about Derek, but how could he when the evidence suggested that Derek was guilty?

"What's up?" asked Leo, hoping that his wife didn't want to engage in a discussion about Derek.

Bypassing the chairs in front of his desk, Vivian walked around behind the massive slab of mahogany wood and sat on his lap.

Startled by the unexpected affection, Leo was about to question her romantic gesture, which he didn't mind and enjoyed very much, but Vivian silenced him with a kiss.

A soulful, lingering kiss that was more intimate than erotic, and which Leo savored and couldn't get enough of and never wanted to end.

Minutes later, she pulled away, smiled and said, "I'm sorry."

Leo frowned. "For kissing me?"

"For letting three days go by without kissing you," said Vivian, pressing her lips against the tip of his nose, and his chin, and above both eyebrows. "I'm sorry for thinking that you're stubborn and unyielding about Derek. I've accused you of not looking at the evidence objectively and letting your feelings about Derek cloud your judgment. I'm sorry that I haven't thought about how hard this situation has been for you. I'm sorry I haven't been more understanding."

Touched by the sincerity in his wife's apology, Leo kissed her, and then said, "I'm sorry, too, babe. I haven't been very willing to see things from your perspective. Honestly, I have been stubborn about my belief in Derek's guilt. I have been unwilling to consider any other possibility because I don't know how to wrap my mind around the concept of Derek being innocent. The Derek I know is always guilty. Or, if not completely guilty, then he's complicit, somehow."

"Derek's always been in trouble of his own making," said Vivian. "I understand that. And I do believe that Derek played a part in this horrible tragedy."

"You just don't think he orchestrated the horrible tragedy," said Leo.

Vivian sighed. "I don't think I have enough facts, at the moment, to make a definitive decision, either way. But, I have to be open to any possibility— even a possibility that I don't believe."

Leo glanced away for a moment, and then said, "Babe, listen, even though I think Derek is guilty, I don't want to think that. You think I don't want to look for evidence that Derek is innocent. I'm afraid that I won't find that evidence if I look for it. I don't want to get my hopes up. People say, hope for the best, but expect the worse. As if you could prepare for the worse. You can't. When the worse happens, it can still destroy you, despite your preparations."

Vivian's hand landed on his jaw, and she leaned toward him, resting her forehead against his.

For a moment, Leo pushed away all the conflicted feelings about Derek and Besi's murder and allowed his wife's touch, and her nearness, to soothe and settle the inner turmoil that had plagued him.

"I have a proposal," said Vivian.

"Let's hear it," said Leo, wrapping his arms around her waist, pulling her closer to him.

"I think we should be open to any possibility," said Vivian. "Right now, we don't know if Derek is guilty or innocent. We have opinions, but let's put those aside. Let's concentrate on getting more facts."

"Sounds good to me," said Leo. "Before you came in here, I was trying to get some facts."

Leaning back to stare at him, Vivian asked, "How?"

"I called Skip Taylor to set up a meeting," said Leo. "Dad keeps hounding me about it, and initially, I resisted, but now I want to hear what Skip has to say."

"When are you going to meet him?"

Running a hand down the back of his head, Leo said, "I haven't set up the meeting. I've been calling him for the past two days, and he hasn't returned my calls."

Vivian frowned. "You think he's avoiding you?"

"At first, I did," said Leo. "Then I told Dad, and he called Skip, but Skip didn't return his calls. Then Derek tried Skip and had no luck. Finally, Dad called Chip Taylor. Chip calls Skip, but the son won't even pick up the phone for his father."

"Skip is avoiding everyone," said Vivian. "Strange."

Leo shrugged and decided not to bring up his thoughts on the matter—namely that Skip wasn't returning the calls because Derek had instructed him to go off the grid. Leo didn't want to risk the rapprochement with his wife by mentioning a theory based on unfounded speculation.

"I've got Stevie looking into whether, or not, Skip left the island," said Leo. "But, he hasn't come up with anything. Maybe we should get Sophie to help him out."

Vivian said, "Speaking of Sophie, she just gave me some information about the brunette. The cops think her name is Elizabeth A. Davis."

"Elizabeth?" Leo frowned. "You think Elizabeth A. Davis might be the Elizabeth that Besi was texting about? The Elizabeth who wasn't going to stay quiet about what she knew?"

"It's possible," said Vivian. "I told Sophie to find out more about Elizabeth A. Davis. So, before we jump to any conclusions, let's see what she comes up with."

"Good idea," Leo said, "By the way, since I accepted your proposal to be open to any possibilities, that means we have an official agreement."

"That we do," she said.

"So, we have to ratify the agreement," he said, slipping his hand beneath her flouncy skirt.

Giggling, Vivian said, "Should we make an announcement? Sign a treaty?"

Sliding his hand between her thighs, Leo kissed her, and said, "I have a better way to seal this deal."

23

"I want to thank you, Burt, for your gracious hospitality during this very difficult time," said Jacob before he glanced at Leo, who sat on the edge of the desk in Burt's spacious home office. "And it was good to see you again, Leo, despite the circumstances."

Nodding, Leo said, "Yeah, you, too."

Earlier during breakfast, Jacob had announced his intentions to leave the island, now that the entire wedding party—excluding Derek—had been cleared to depart St. Killian.

Leo didn't blame the guy. Who wanted to stay in a paradise marred by the death of the bride and the subsequent arrest of the groom? Zeke and Tom York had skipped town yesterday, and Kelsea was jetting off tomorrow when one of the private planes in her father's fleet would arrive to whisk her away. Melanie, however, had decided to stick around. She claimed she wanted to see if Besi would get the justice she deserved, but Leo suspected, with her employer and best friend dead, Melanie had nowhere to go.

"Of course," said Burt, "and you are welcome. I'm just so very sorry that such a horrific tragedy ruined your time on this beautiful island."

Jacob let out a breath. "I still can't believe that Besi was killed and Derek …"

Though he knew what Jacob had been about to say, Leo stayed quiet, deciding to spare his father any sardonic quips. None of the wedding party could believe that Derek had been arrested for taking out a contract on Besi's life.

Before Vivian's article about the announcement of Aaron Jones as the man who'd killed Besi at Derek's request, Burt had given himself the task of informing the wedding party of Derek's arrest. Leo was thankful his dad did the honors, considering Tom's vindictive outburst. Declaring that he'd been right about Derek, Tom expressed no surprise that Derek was accused of putting a hit out on Besi. Kelsea, Jacob, Zeke, and Melanie had been shocked, but solemn.

Clearing his throat, Burt asked, "What time is your flight?"

"Later this afternoon," said Jacob. "Around six o'clock."

Three more hours, thought Leo as he glanced at his watch, and then Jacob could put all this trouble in paradise behind him. A spark of envy flared within Leo. What he wouldn't give to be free of having to deal with the mess Derek had made. Instead of leaving the island, Leo had to search for Skip Taylor. Which reminded him that he needed to call Stevie for an update on Taylor's whereabouts.

"Well, if there is anything you need before you go," began Burt, "please let Lemuel know, and—"

"Actually, um, before I go." Jacob's shoulders slumped as he glanced at the carpet. "There's something I need to tell you. Something important, but ..."

"But?" Leo prompted.

Jacob sighed and looked up. A hint of panic crossed his features as he said, "I don't want to get Derek in trouble."

Leo felt something like alarm bells imploding within him, but he forced himself to remain calm and remember what he'd promised Vivian. They'd made a pact to consider all possibilities and not jump to conclusions. He would wait and hear Jacob out before he automatically assumed the worse.

"Jacob, I think you'd better tell us what you have to say," said Burt, his tone polite, and yet commanding.

After a shaky breath, Jacob said, "Now that Derek has been implicated in Besi's murder, I think I need to tell you."

"Tell us what?" asked Burt.

"Derek is going to inherit Besi's entire fortune," said Jacob, glancing down.

"What the hell are you talking about?" Leo demanded.

Jacob glanced up, his gaze darting from Burt to Leo, and said, "Five years ago, when Besi turned twenty-one, she came into possession of a five-hundred-million-dollar trust. That money will transfer to Derek, as soon as Besi's will is probated."

"How do you know this?" Leo asked.

"My dad is Besi's attorney," said Jacob. "A month after Besi and Derek got engaged, Besi went to Dad and told him she wanted to change her will. Dad didn't think it was a good idea and he asked me to convince Besi not to make any changes."

"But, you weren't able to convince Besi," said Burt, pinching the bridge of his nose.

"What did Besi say when you told her not to change her will?" Leo asked.

"She and Derek had come to some kind of pre-marital agreement," said Jacob. "The deal was, if Derek signed a prenuptial agreement, then Besi would change her will."

Leo stared at Jacob. "You're kidding."

Jacob shook his head. "Besi told me that she didn't mind changing her will because Derek signed the prenup, which said that if Derek was caught cheating on her and the allegations were conclusively proven, then Besi could divorce Derek, he would get no spousal support, and the provision in her will for him would be immediately nullified."

Burt exhaled.

"Unbelievable," said Leo. "But, wait a minute. Derek and Besi didn't get married. How can he inherit her money if he's not her husband?"

"Besi changed her will last year after she and Derek got engaged," said Jacob. "The beneficiary is Derek Hennessy. There's no provision in the will that says Derek has to be her husband to inherit her money."

"Why am I not surprised?" asked Leo, feeling as though he'd just been sucker-punched in the nuts. "That's why Derek had Besi killed."

"Leonard, please," warned Burt.

"He had five hundred million reasons," said Leo, flabbergasted.

Jacob cleared his throat. "I don't know if Derek had Besi killed, or not. I just thought you should know about Besi's will."

Burt said, "Jacob, thank you for informing us."

Following Jacob's departure from the office, Leo stared at his father. "I think you need to come to terms with the possibility that, considering what Jacob told us about Besi's will, Derek hired Jones to kill her."

Burt stared back at him, steel blue eyes unyielding and unwavering. "Why should I consider such a ridiculous possibility?"

Leo shook his head. "You still think Derek is innocent?"

Burt exhaled. "Leonard—"

"Why are you so hell-bent on seeing the best in Derek?"

"Because no one else does, or ever has, bothered to see anything worthwhile or redeeming in Derek," said Burt. "And someone has to."

Leo frowned. "Dad, get real."

"I know you don't think that Derek deserves the benefit of our doubt, let alone our compassion, or sympathy—"

"Sympathy?" Leo snorted. "You want me to feel sorry for Derek? Dad, the guy had his fiancée killed so he could inherit half-a-billion dollars."

"I don't believe that," his father said. "Is Derek a saint? Absolutely not. Far from it, I know that. But, is he a heartless, cold-blooded murderer?"

"Yeah, Dad, I think he just might be a heartless, cold-blooded murderer," Leo said.

Burt exhaled and sat back. "Leonard, despite what you may think, I don't need you to feel sorry for Derek. What I need are your exemplary investigative skills. Derek is being framed. I need you to find out who had Besi killed."

"You sure about that?" quipped Leo, crossing his arms. "I didn't exactly do such a great job finding evidence to prove Winnie's innocence."

"Leonard—"

"Forget it," said Leo, frustrated by his father's willingness to ignore the truth about Derek. "You want Derek's name cleared? Do it yourself."

24

Placing the bottle of red polish on the bedtable, Vivian decided to forget about touching up her toenails and concentrate on her husband, who paced back and forth, his fists clenched, jaw muscles tensed.

Moments ago, Leo entered the guest bedroom and slammed the door behind him. Looking like contents under pressure, ready to explode, he stalked from the bed to the wardrobe and back to the bed.

"What's the matter?" asked Vivian, swinging her legs over the side of the bed.

Leo stopped pacing and stared at her. "Derek has a motive for killing Besi."

Standing, Vivian frowned as she walked toward him. "He does?"

Dropping down on the settee at the foot of the bed, Leo shook his head. "You're not going to believe this."

Joining him on the settee, Vivian listened in rapt attention as Leo revealed the details of a conversation between himself, Burt, and Jacob concerning the last will and testament of Besi Beaumont.

"I'm more convinced than ever that Derek hired Jones to kill Besi," said Leo. "Dad doesn't believe it, of course. He wants me to clear Derek's name. Can you believe him? How the hell am I supposed to do that when I don't believe that Derek is innocent? This crap Derek told us about being blackmailed by Aaron Jones is bullshit."

"Are you sure it's bullshit?" asked Vivian.

Dragging a hand down the side of his face, Leo said, "Let's say it's true. What does Jones have on Derek?"

"Maybe something to do with Derek's gambling," suggested Vivian. "Or, maybe Jones knew why Derek was fired from Hennessy Capital."

Leo shook his head. "Why would Derek pay a guy to stay quiet about why he was fired? Losing his job is embarrassing, but who cares if someone finds out why?"

Turning toward Leo, Vivian tucked one leg beneath the other. "Derek said his life would be ruined if people knew why he was let go. Hennessy Capital is an investment firm. Maybe he mismanaged one of their client's money? Or, what if Derek used client money to gamble?"

Still unconvinced, Leo asked, "How could Jones have found out why Derek was fired?"

"Someone must have told him," said Vivian. "Derek isn't the only one who knows why he was fired."

"David Hennessy knows why," said Leo. "But, I doubt he told Jones. I'm sure he doesn't know the guy."

"Someone at the company might have known Derek was fired for mismanaging funds," said Vivian. "That someone might be Elizabeth A. Davis."

"The brunette in the sunglasses?"

Picking up on the doubt in her husband's tone, Vivian said, "Hear me out first before you shoot down my theories."

Leo exhaled. "I'm listening."

"What if Elizabeth A. Davis works at Hennessy Capital. Maybe in HR or Legal. A department where she might get wind of why Derek was fired," said Vivian. "Maybe she wants to expose Derek, or embarrass him or, just cash in on his misfortune."

"Derek didn't say anything about being blackmailed by Elizabeth Davis," said Leo.

"Elizabeth can't risk contacting Derek herself with a blackmail demand. So, maybe she gets her friend Aaron Jones to help her," said Vivian. "Jones contacts Derek and tells him that he wants money, or he'll expose what Derek did to get himself fired."

"If Elizabeth Davis was secretly blackmailing Derek," said Leo, "then maybe she's not the Elizabeth that Besi was texting about not staying quiet."

"Maybe Jones let it slip that Elizabeth was involved," said Vivian, though she worried her theory had loose ends which were starting to unravel. "So then maybe Skip, and Besi were involved at that point. The fiancée and the fixer arranged to pay off Elizabeth, but maybe Elizabeth wasn't going to stay quiet unless they gave her more money."

Leo asked, "You think the mystery burner phone belongs to Skip and Besi was texting him when she was in the Aerie Islands? And the problem with Elizabeth is that she wanted a bigger payout?"

Vivian nodded. "Just when Besi and Skip think they've fixed the situation, Elizabeth wants a larger payout. Jones might have convinced Elizabeth to ask for more cash."

"Okay, let's go with your theory that Derek did something that would be considered a crime, Elizabeth Davis found out, and got Jones to help her blackmail Derek," said Leo. "If Derek paid Jones and Elizabeth, then why would Jones kill Besi?"

"Maybe because Jones and Elizabeth didn't get what they wanted," said Vivian. "Jones and Elizabeth might have threatened to kill Besi if they didn't get more cash. Maybe they made good on that threat."

25

"Tell me again why I hired Stevie," requested Leo, closing the door after he crossed the threshold into Vivian's office.

Turning from her computer, Vivian grabbed the cup of coffee sitting on her desk calendar and took a sip. "What's he done now?"

"Nothing," said Leo, dropping down onto the couch. "That's the problem. He still hasn't found Skip Taylor, and I don't think he's giving it his all. Although, admittedly, his all isn't much. Are you sure Sophie doesn't have time to help him?"

"Speaking of Sophie," said Vivian, sitting the coffee cup down. "I was right about hiring her. She's shaping up to be a pretty good investigator."

"What's she done now?"

"Sophie talked to Officer Fields last night," said Vivian, anxious to share the news Sophie had been champing at the bit to tell her. When Vivian arrived at the paper around eight that morning, the junior reporter had been waiting outside her office, barely unable to contain the news.

"Last night?" asked Leo. "She doesn't expect overtime, does she?"

"Since when is journalism a nine-to-five job," said Vivian, rolling her eyes. "Anyway, Sophie saw Fields at a bar, and they started talking. Fields was off duty and on his third Felipe beer, according to Sophie, when he told her that the AR-15 used to kill Besi is a PC-5 ghost gun."

"A ghost gun," said Leo. "Unregistered and untraceable."

Nodding, Vivian said, "Some of the lower level members make extra money selling illegal guns. They buy the rifle parts unfinished online to avoid attracting law enforcement, then make the guns in machine shops."

Leo shook his head. "The PC-5 is indirectly responsible for Besi's death."

"The gang is indirectly responsible for most of the crime in the Palmchat Islands, which is a shame," opined Vivian. "Most people don't even realize that the PC-5 was originally a civil rights organization. The five founders wanted independence. They wanted clean drinking water, access to better schools, decent hospitals. They weren't about killing people and trafficking drugs and selling ghost guns."

"I think you're giving the O.G.'s too much credit," said Leo. "They used civil disobedience in their fight for those civil rights."

"And so what if they did?" challenged Vivian. "The way I see it, they had no other choice."

"They did what they had to do, I agree," said Leo. "But, you know, the founders made deals with drug cartels for guns that they used to hold the island hostage until they got independence."

"Be that as it may," said Vivian, irritated by her husband's unwillingness to sympathize with the plight of the marginalized and disenfranchised. "My point was that the PC-5 was not created to be a violent, ruthless island gang but that's what they've become, unfortunately."

"True, but when you decide that a certain goal must be accomplished no matter the cost," said Leo, "then you have to be prepared to pay the price when the goal is accomplished."

Feeling her blood pressure rising, Vivian said, "So, you're saying the price for independence was what? Illegal enterprise?"

Shrugging, Leo said, "They won independence with violence, so ..."

"So?" demanded Vivian.

Leo cleared his throat. "Well—"

A quick knock on the door interrupted him.

"Come in," called out Leo.

Seconds later, when the door opened, Vivian took note of the relief on her husband's face as Roland "Beanie" Bean, a senior reporter at the *Palmchat Gazette* walked into her office. Vivian was glad Beanie's interruption had brought it to an abrupt end before their debate turned into an argument.

"Don't mean to bother you," said Beanie.

"It's no bother," said Leo. "What do you need?"

"I have information about the ghost gun that killed Besi Beaumont," said Beanie. "Sophie sent me a text about it last night, so I decided to reach out to one of my Handweg contacts, find out if he knew anything."

"And did he?" asked Vivian, her irritation with Leo subsiding as her interest in the ghost gun reignited.

"The gun used to kill Besi was bought by a white guy," said Beanie. "My contact didn't know the buyer's name, but the guy paid for the gun with a six-figure Rolex watch. The PC-5 thug who accepted the watch as payment fenced it to a shady jeweler who runs a gold and diamond exchange."

"Aaron Jones must be the guy who bought the gun from the PC-5 member," said Vivian.

"Where did he get the Rolex to pay for it?" Leo asked.

Beanie said, "Maybe he got it from Derek Hennessy."

"Why do you say that?" Leo asked.

"According to my contact," said Beanie. "There was a name engraved on the watch."

"Don't tell me," said Leo.

Beanie said, "Derek was engraved on the back of the Rolex."

26

"A Rolex watch?" Confusion in his gaze, Derek shook his head as he looked up from the wedge of pound cake, covered in mango compote, on his dessert plate. "I don't have a Rolex watch."

"Are you sure?" asked Leo, glaring at Derek, who sat directly across from him at the table in the informal dining salon.

Dinner had been, as usual, reserved, if not somber, with superficial conversation designed to avoid more controversial topics.

"What are these questions about a Rolex watch?" asked Burt, sitting at the head of the table.

"That's what I'd like to know," said Vivian, an edge of admonition in her tone. Earlier, after their conversation with Beanie about the watch, he and Viv had decided to verify the story before questioning Derek about the Rolex. A glance at his wife confirmed her annoyance with him for going off script.

Leo would risk her irritation. After they'd been unable to talk to the jeweler, who'd had to close his shop early due to an unforeseen family emergency, he'd concluded that he didn't need verification. He needed answers from Derek. The dessert course, he figured, was as good a time as any for an interrogation.

Clutching his fork, Derek shook his head. "I don't have a Rolex."

"That's ... that's not true," said Melanie, staring at Derek, who sat next to her. "You're lying."

Derek gaped at her. "What the hell—"

"You do have a Rolex," said Melanie. "Besi bought it for you. I was with her when she bought it, and she told me she was going to give it to you after she came back from the Aerie Islands."

"Besi never gave me a Rolex watch," said Derek.

"That's not true!" Melanie shouted, rattling the silver utensils and plates as she banged her fists against the table. "Why do you keep lying? Why don't you tell the truth? You had Besi killed! You never loved her! You only wanted her money!"

"I did love Besi," Derek insisted. "I wanted to spend the rest of my life with her!"

"You mean you wanted to spend the rest of your life with her money," said Leo.

"She never should have gotten involved with you!" Melanie pushed back from the table and jumped up. "You made her change her will! You made her get plastic surgery! But, that wasn't enough! She met all your demands, and you still killed her!"

His face a mask of stricken shock, Derek stuttered his denial. "Mel, I didn't—"

"You evil bastard!" Melanie whacked Derek across the face.

The force of the blow, which sent Melanie stumbling from momentum, stunned Leo. Next to him, Vivian jumped slightly.

"Melanie," bellowed Burt. "Calm yourself. Please."

Her face flushed and blotchy, Melanie burst into heaving sobs.

"Vivian," said Burt. "Can you see about Melanie?"

"Sure," said Vivian, rising from her seat. Walking to Melanie, Vivian put her arm around the hysterical woman and led her out of the room.

Scowling, his face lobster red, Derek sat motionlessly, jaws clenched and fists in a tight ball.

Burt said, "Leonard, what is going on with this Rolex watch?"

Leo said, "Derek can explain—"

"I want answers right now!" Burt thundered.

Disappointed by his father's withering glare, Leo repeated the information Beanie had shared with him and Vivian earlier that morning.

Burt asked, "Did you confirm that the Rolex watch has 'Derek' engraved on the back case?"

"Melanie just confirmed it," said Leo. "Did you not hear her?"

"Melanie said that Besi bought a Rolex watch for Derek," said Burt. "There was no mention of the watch being engraved."

"I can't believe you!" Leo said. "Why are you so damned determined to ignore all the evidence? Why do you refuse to accept the truth?"

"Why are you so damned determined to believe I'm guilty?" Derek asked Leo. "Melanie is wrong. Besi never gave me a watch after she got back from her surgery in the Aerie Islands."

"So, you're saying Melanie lied?" asked Leo.

"Derek said that Melanie was wrong," said Burt. "I believe that, as well. I don't dispute that Besi bought Derek a watch, but I don't think she gave it to him."

"Then how did the watch end up in a gold and diamond shop in downtown St. Killian?" asked Leo. "How did the watch end up as payment for the gun used to kill Besi?"

"I have no idea," said Derek, a forlorn weariness in his tone. "Maybe someone stole the watch from Besi."

"Leo, I'd like you to look into this situation with the Rolex watch," said Burt.

"And talk to Skip," said Derek.

"Yeah, I would if I could," said Leo, standing. "But, for some reason, Skip Taylor isn't returning my calls."

27

Approaching the storefront, Leo checked out the tasteful display of gold and diamonds behind large, plate-glass windows of the Luxury Gold and Diamond Emporium, located on the far east end of downtown.

According to Beanie's source in Handweg, this was the place where the Rolex watch engraved with Derek's name had been fenced. Tracking down the shady jeweler had been fairly easy, considering that there was only one gold and diamond exchange in St. Killian.

Removing his Ray Bans, Leo walked into the store. The frosty air conditioning was a welcome respite from the brutal sun and humidity that nearly smothered him as he made the five-block walk from the *Palmchat Gazette* offices.

Leo glanced around the shop. Typical jewelry store. He could think of better ways to waste a Tuesday afternoon, but he was determined to prove that Derek had given the watch to Aaron Jones as payment for the AR-15 ghost gun.

Behind a waist-high glass display counter, a balding, fifty-something Southeast Asian man tried to convince a couple of tourists dressed alike in khaki shorts and T-shirts declaring their love for the Palmchat Islands, why they should purchase a diamond tennis bracelet.

The jeweler nodded to Leo, deftly acknowledging him while continuing to hawk his glittery wares to the couple. Leo doubted they were sincerely interested. Sweaty, flushed, and fanning themselves with small, folded street maps, they were probably more interested in the A/C than the bling.

Moments later, not surprisingly, the couple left without making a purchase. The jeweler had given them a conciliatory smile, but when they turned, he'd pursed his lips as he returned the tennis bracelet.

"My friend! Good day, and how are you," said the jeweler, his smile once again magnanimous. "How can I help you today?"

Leo wasted no time inquiring about purchasing a Rolex watch.

"You are in luck, my friend," said the jeweler, a hint of an English accent in his engaging tone. "I have four that you can choose from. Now, I will be honest with you … "

Leo doubted it, but he tried to keep his expression pleasant as he waited for the guy to continue.

"One of the watches have engravings on the case backs," said the jeweler. "Of course, some people like engravings because they give the piece character, but I can get new case backs if you prefer. Won't be a problem at all."

Shrugging, Leo said, "I don't mind engravings. Depends on what it says. Initials are okay, but I don't need words of wisdom or professions of love."

The owner sighed. "Well, then you might not be interested in my latest acquisition, which is the nicest watch in my possession at the moment, but it has a very personalized engraving. The other three Rolexes don't—"

"I'd like to see it," said Leo. "If the engraving is too mushy, I could get another case back. If the watch is as nice as you claim it is."

"Oh, my friend, it is very, very nice," said the jeweler. "I received it a week, or so, ago, from a man who no longer desired it, though he didn't tell me why, but that doesn't matter. Wait here. I have the watch in the back. I'll bring it out to show you."

As the jeweler scurried off, Leo's pulse jumped. Mulling over the owner's description of the Rolex, with its personalized engraving, he drummed his fingers against the glass counter. Was it the same Rolex Besi had bought Derek for a wedding gift? The Rolex he claimed she'd never given him? The Rolex that Aaron Jones had used as payment for an AR-15 ghost gun?

Leo suspected he was about to verify the story from Beanie's source, but he wasn't sure he wanted to. Part of him, for some reason, hoped the watch would bear no mention of Derek. Leo exhaled, anxious for the jeweler to return.

Minutes later, after the jeweler showed him the engraving on the case back of the Rolex, Leo stared at the etching, his heart pounding as several emotions coursed through him.

"What do you think, my friend?" asked the jeweler. "You like the watch?"

"Thanks, but, no," said Leo. "Don't think this is the right watch for me."

Ignoring the jeweler's attempt to show him a different watch, Leo turned and hurried out of the store. Donning his sunglasses, he walked away from the Luxury Gold and Diamond Emporium, the image of the case back engraved in his mind: *Derek, I will love you always. Besi.*

28

An hour later, back in his office, Leo decided to go over notes for an upcoming meeting with the Bronson Publishing lawyers next week. There was no need to prepare himself so far in advance, but he needed the distraction. A long, laborious overseas conference call would have been perfect right about now, but he didn't have one scheduled. There weren't many tasks on his calendar today. Nothing important or time-sensitive. Nothing to take his mind off that damn Rolex watch engraved with Derek's name.

Once again, Derek had lied.

But, this time, Leo wasn't sure how to deal with the deception. Normally, he wouldn't be surprised, but confirming the story from Beanie's source about the Rolex presented Leo with another set of ramifications and potential consequences, all of them dire.

Leo sighed and leaned back in his chair. He would have to tell his father about the trip to the gold and diamond exchange. He wasn't looking forward to that. What would his father think? How would Burt react? More blind loyalty and unwavering belief in Derek's innocence? Or, a grudging realization of Derek's dishonesty and cold-blooded brutality?

Gazing out of the ceiling-to-floor plate glass windows, which offered a view of downtown St. Killian, Leo struggled to come to terms with Derek's guilt. He'd always been suspicious of Derek, but now that he'd discovered evidence to prove his suspicions, he wasn't sure how he felt.

A percussive knock on his door interrupted his musings.

Stevie Bishop peeped around the door. "Hey, boss, got a sec?"

Normally, Stevie was the last person Leo wanted to deal with.

Stevie, whose last name was associated with wealth and privilege in the Palmchat Islands, had been hired by Burt as a favor to Stevie's father, the founder of a multi-billion-dollar brewing conglomerate. As far as Leo was concerned, Stevie had been handed a job he wasn't interested in, a job which should have gone to a more deserving candidate. Since he couldn't fire Stevie, Leo had grudgingly decided to mentor him, though he could barely tolerate Stevie's nonchalant surfer dude attitude.

Right now, he hoped the slacker-reporter could distract him from his worrisome thoughts about Derek.

"I got a minute, or two," said Leo. "What do you need?"

"Got some news about Skip Taylor," said Stevie, walking into the office.

Tension coiled in Leo's gut. So much for distraction from Stevie. Despite giving the slacker-reporter the task of finding Taylor, Leo hadn't thought Stevie would come through with any useful information. He certainly wasn't in the mood to discuss anyone with any connection to Derek Hennessy.

"He hasn't left the island." Stevie dropped down in the chair in front of Leo's desk.

Hesitant, Leo asked, "Are you sure?"

Stevie frowned. "Pretty sure. I found out from some friends who work at the airport that when Skip Taylor arrived on the island, he rented a car from St. Killian Car Rentals. A Toyota Camry. Then, instead of checking into a hotel, he rented a house in Oyster Farms. Far as I know, he's still there, but I didn't go by the house and confirm that. Guess I should have, huh?"

A hint of a memory sparked within Leo. "A house in Oyster Farms?"

"On Dove Street," said Stevie.

Rubbing his jaw, Leo said, "Are you sure?"

"Huh? I mean, yeah, I'm sure." Stevie frowned. "I think so. Wait. Let me check my notes."

"Don't bother," Leo said, reaching toward his desk phone. Pressing the button that connected him to Vivian's office, Leo requested his wife's presence.

Minutes later, Vivian stood in the doorway. "What is it? I have a meeting with the news staff in ten minutes."

"Should I be at that meeting?" asked Stevie.

Leo tried not to laugh as Vivian glared at Stevie.

"Aren't you part of the news staff?" demanded Vivian.

"Yeah," said Stevie, as though some revelation had dawned on him. "I guess I am."

Clearing his throat, Leo said, "Stevie just confirmed that Skip Taylor did rent that house on Dove Street. The bastard is hiding out, or laying low, in Oyster Farms."

Stevie said, "Wait, you already knew about the house on Dove Street?"

"We suspected Skip Taylor might have rented the house," said Vivian. "We believe Besi Beaumont went to see Skip at the rental house the Tuesday before she was killed."

"Now that you've confirmed our suspicions," said Leo, sitting forward. "We can find out what Skip has to say about his meeting with Besi."

29

"Maybe Besi didn't go to see Skip Taylor," said Vivian, rolling down the window of Leo's old Ford truck as he shifted into park and cut the engine. "As you pointed out when we found out the address programmed into the BMW's GPS, we couldn't conclusively determine whether or not Besi had driven to the rental house on Dove Street."

Leo shook his head. "If she didn't drive to Skip Taylor's rental house, then why did she put the Dove Street address in the GPS? Before we left, Stevie confirmed that there's only one Dove Street in St. Killian."

"I know that," said Vivian, concerned by her husband's clenched jaw and dogged determination. "But, maybe—"

"I came here to talk to Skip Taylor, and that's what I'm going to do," said Leo, opening the driver's door. "He can tell me if Besi came to see him, and if she did, he's going to tell me why."

Leo stepped out of the truck and slammed the door.

Vivian jumped and then exhaled as she glanced at her watch. A few minutes after two o'clock. Right now, she should have been developing and assigning story ideas for her reporting staff. She'd canceled the meeting when Leo insisted on driving to Oyster Farms to question Skip Taylor. Her husband hadn't asked her to tag along, but Leo's confrontational tone bothered her. She worried that the meeting with the fixer would become contentious, considering Leo's hostile demeanor.

Exiting the Ford, Vivian closed the door as Leo headed around the front of the truck and up the driveway of the rental house on Dove Street.

Vivian took a deep breath and hurried to follow her husband. Striding past the Toyota Camry, she frowned. As Leo had driven to the house in Oyster Farms, Vivian had hoped that Skip Taylor would be gone, but no such luck. Joining Leo at the front door of the modest home, Vivian asked, "What's your game plan? More flies with honey than vinegar?"

Usually, Leo's interviewing techniques involved finding some way to sympathize or find some common ground with a witness. His approach relied on a principle that people were more likely to open up to someone who was compassionate and kind, than to a person coming at them with a barrage of questions. No one wanted to be interrogated, especially by a reporter with no reason to expect, or demand, answers.

"Might have to use brute force," said Leo. "If Taylor opens the damn door, which it doesn't seem likely."

"Maybe he's not home," suggested Vivian, her concern increasing as Leo banged on the door.

Hearing a car drive by, she glanced over her shoulder. The last thing they needed was some nosey neighbor thinking they were trying to break into the house and calling the cops.

"The car he rented is in the driveway," said Leo. "He's home. Probably peering at me through the peephole."

"But, maybe—"

"I'm going around to the backyard," said Leo, leaving the front porch.

"You think you should?" asked Vivian, following him around to the side of the house. Shaded from the afternoon sun by the roof, the narrow path leading to the backyard separated the rental home from the house next to it.

Leo said nothing as he strode through the grass and stopped at the wooden gate.

"I don't think this is a good idea," said Vivian, walking up behind him. "This is private property. We can't just—"

"Look at this," said Leo, stepping aside. "There's some damage to the gate."

Beneath the chest-high lock, which seemed to be bent, several planks were broken, the wooden boards splintered and nearly split apart.

"Maybe someone tried to break into the house," said Vivian, curiosity overtaking her concern.

"Maybe," said Leo as he pulled the gate open and headed into the backyard.

Besides two large hibiscus bushes against the back fence, there wasn't much landscaping and the grass, ankle high, needed attention.

As they walked up the steps to the back deck, Leo said, "Check out the patio door."

Vivian took a deep breath. The right pane of the double-side sliding glass patio door was completely shattered. Shards and slivers of glass jutted from the metal frame while chunks littered the deck and the tile floor inside the house.

The left side of the door sent a chill through Vivian.

Two small holes in the glass, about five inches apart, had broken the wide pane, cracking the glass into the "spider's web" effect.

"Guess someone did break in," said Vivian.

"What's that on the glass?" Leo crossed the wooden planks to get a closer look at the shattered patio door. Standing behind Leo, Vivian gasped as she gazed at the image on the left glass pane, several inches above the small holes.

A faded, rust-colored handprint.

30

"Detective, I was going to call you," said Vivian, smiling as Baxter François walked into her office.

"Guess I saved you the trouble," said the detective, taking a seat in one of the chairs in front of her desk.

"Wouldn't have been any trouble," said Vivian. "I'm glad you stopped by. I have some questions for you."

"Great minds think alike, as they say," quipped Detective François. "I have some questions for you, as well, about the trip you and your lesser half took to a house on Dove Street in Oyster Farms yesterday afternoon."

Grabbing a red editing pen from the coffee mug near the corner of her desk, Vivian tried to prepare herself for the detective's inquiry, which she'd been expecting.

After she and Leo had discovered the broken fence gate, shattered patio door, and faint handprint on the glass pane, they'd called the police. While waiting for the St. Killian deputies, they'd debated what they would admit to the police concerning their reason for being at the Dove Street house. Vivian thought they should come clean with the truth. Leo wanted to stay as close to the truth as possible without revealing their true motives. Eventually, they decided to tell the cops that they were following up on a lead about a robbery. The deputies looked skeptical but released them to leave with a warning that they might be asked to come to the station for follow-up questions.

"What a coincidence," said Vivian. "I have questions for you about the house on Dove Street. Specifically, was that rust-colored handprint blood? And were those bullet holes in the glass?"

The detective smiled and then said, "We'll get to that. First, why were you and your husband at that house?"

"We told the deputy—"

"If you want to know more about that rust-colored handprint on the glass," began the detective, "then I suggest you tell me the truth."

Vivian exhaled. She knew she couldn't fool Detective François. Why she always tried, she didn't know. "We were looking for a guy named Skip Taylor. Leo wanted to talk to him."

"About?"

"Maybe you should ask Leo that," said Vivian, unable to resist toying with the detective.

"Reason I want to know," said François, "is because I have some information about Skip Taylor."

Trying to mask her surprise, Vivian asked, "What do you know about Skip Taylor?"

"What did your husband want to talk to Taylor about?"

Vivian tapped the editing pen against her cheek. "Derek claims Skip Taylor can prove he had nothing to do with Besi Beaumont's murder. Leo wanted to find out if that's true. But Skip Taylor wasn't around."

Fixing her with a pensive stare, the detective asked, "What was going on with Skip Taylor, Aaron Jones, and Derek?"

"What do you mean?" Vivian asked, stalling for time. She wasn't sure what the detective was trying to coax out of her, but she knew she'd have to be careful with her responses.

The detective said, "I'm going to tell you what I know, and you can fill in some of the gaps for me. How about that?"

"I'll try," said Vivian. "But, I may not be able to help you."

"I appreciate your effort," said François, reaching into his jacket and pulling out a phone. "Let me just consult my notes."

Concerned and curious, Vivian waited.

"So, it appears that," the detective said, staring at his phone, "Skip Taylor made several phone calls and sent text messages to Aaron Jones regarding Derek Hennessy. What do you know about that?"

Knowing that she wasn't in a position to reveal what she knew about Derek's relationship to the fixer, Vivian asked, "How do you know that Skip Taylor made phone calls to Aaron Jones?"

"We have Aaron Jones' cell phone," said François. "Remember, that's how we saw the messages between Jones and Derek Hennessy. So, I know how Jones and Hennessy are connected. But, what does Skip Taylor have to do with all of this? How does he know Derek Hennessy?"

"Did you ask Derek about Skip Taylor?"

"After his arrest," said François, "Mr. Hennessy refused to talk and lawyered up immediately. He has yet to make an official statement. His dream team claims they plan to make their client available for questioning but to tell you the truth, I'm not in the mood to deal with a dozen defense attorneys advising Mr. Hennessy not to answer any of my questions."

"Then maybe you should ask Skip Taylor?" Vivian suggested. "That is if you can find him."

"Oh, I know exactly where Mr. Taylor is," said François.

"Where is he?" Vivian asked, wondering if the detective would tell her.

"You remember that story you published about a guy who'd been shot and then hit by a car in Oyster Farms?" asked the detective. "Taylor's the guy who was shot and hit by a car."

Stunned, Vivian stared at him. "Are you serious?"

"Skip Taylor is in the hospital," said the detective. "I went there to question him about Mr. Hennessy, but it didn't go so well."

"Taylor refused to talk?" asked Vivian.

"Skip Taylor can't tell me anything," said François. "He's got amnesia."

31

"Amnesia, my ass," muttered Leo as he entered St. Killian General Hospital.

Cold and yet balmy, the sterile atmosphere held a faint hint of bleach that couldn't quite cover the stench of sickness and disease.

On the second floor, Leo exited the elevator and headed down the hall, striding casually, hoping to appear as a family member visiting a sick relative. Last thing he wanted was to arouse suspicions as he meandered among the nurses, doctors, and patients ambling slowly, clutching IV poles. Didn't want anyone to know that he planned to get the truth from Skip Taylor, one way or the other.

Whatever it took, Leo was determined to jog the fixer's memory.

Not that he believed Taylor had amnesia, despite the injuries that purportedly caused his memory loss. Leo was quite certain that Skip Taylor hadn't forgotten anything.

When Vivian had shared the incredulous story last night over dinner with Burt and Derek, Leo had been skeptical. Initially, Burt was surprised but was willing to believe that a gunshot wound could cause memory loss. Derek, wild-eyed and surprised, thought the amnesia explained the fixer's absence and avoidance.

Leo hadn't bought Derek's shock.

After he and Vivian discussed the matter in private, his wife had encouraged him to keep an open mind and not jump to conclusions.

The fixer didn't deserve the benefit of the doubt, as far as Leo was concerned.

Walking past the nurse's station, Leo slowed as an orderly pushing an old man in a wheelchair crossed his path and into one of the hospital rooms. Number 212. Skip Taylor was in Room 218, according to Stevie, who'd gotten the information from a friend who worked at the hospital.

Leo's pulse quickened as he passed Room 214 and then Room 216.

He did not doubt that Derek and Skip had come up with this bullshit amnesia story so Skip wouldn't have to answer any questions about the role he'd played in Besi's murder.

And yet, when Leo approached Room 218, he hesitated. Bothered by a strange doubt, he stared at the closed hospital door. Since his arrest, Derek had sworn that Skip Taylor would corroborate his claims about being blackmailed by Aaron Jones. So, why would Derek tell Skip to fake amnesia? Derek needed Skip to lie to the cops. How could the fixer prove Derek's innocence if he couldn't remember anything?

Ignoring the doubts, Leo opened the door and stepped into the room.

Reclining in the hospital bed, the fixer looked like he was relaxing on a chaise lounge at a luxury spa resort. As he chuckled at the syndicated talk show playing on the television mounted on the wall across from the bed, Skip Taylor didn't appear to be recovering from being shot and then hit by a car.

"How you doing, Skip?" asked Leo, certain the fixer had seen him but was ignoring him on purpose.

"Who the hell are you?" asked Taylor, his gaze focused on the talk show antics.

"You know who I am," said Leo, staring at Taylor.

The fixer stared at him. "What do you want?"

"I want the truth," said Leo. "Derek was arrested for putting a hit out on Besi, but he says he's being framed. The cops have evidence that he hired Aaron Jones to carry out the hit. Derek claims the cops have it all wrong. Derek says Jones was blackmailing him and that you fixed everything. So, that's what I want to know, Skip. How did you fix things?"

Taylor smiled, but Leo thought it looked more like a grimace.

"You know I got amnesia, right?" said Taylor, focusing on the television again. "Doctors say I can't remember nothing. Not even my name. But, doctors don't know everything, do they?"

"What do you know?" asked Leo, quite certain that Taylor was talking in code.

"What I know is that, in an hour or so, I'll be headed outside to walk around the lake behind the hospital," said the fixer. "Part of my physical therapy routine. It's a nice lake. Palm trees. Ducks in the water. Nice place to have a conversation."

Understanding what Taylor wanted him to do, Leo said, "I like ducks. Maybe I'll go out to the lake and feed them."

32

Pebbly pea gravel crunched beneath Leo's Italian leather driving shoes as he strode down the path that ran along the perimeter of the small, man-made lake behind the hospital.

Staring at lily pads floating on the lake's placid surface, Leo checked his watch.

Fifteen more minutes and Skip Taylor would be heading out to the lake for his afternoon walk. Or, he *should* be headed down to the lake. Leo didn't trust Taylor. He wouldn't be surprised if the fixer didn't show up, but the trip hadn't been in vain. He was fairly certain he'd been right about Taylor. The amnesia claim was a ruse. But, why?

Leo walked toward one of several benches, surrounded by hibiscus bushes and date palm trees, positioned along the path. Taking a seat, he focused on two ducks splashing in the water.

Why would Derek want Skip to fake amnesia? Didn't make sense. Unless the fake amnesia was Skip's idea. Again, why?

The way Leo figured it, Skip fixed the situation by hiring Aaron Jones to kill Besi, thus ensuring that Derek would inherit her fortune before Besi kicked him to the curb. Then, Skip fixed the situation with Aaron Jones by killing the hitman so he wouldn't cause problems in the future.

Leo supposed it was possible Skip Taylor thought he might be next on

Derek's hit list. Maybe he was faking amnesia as a message to Derek that he wasn't a rat.

"This seat taken?"

Recognizing the guttural, East-coast accent, Leo glanced up.

"Not that I'm aware of," said Leo, anxious to find out what the fixer had to say, and yet wary of getting his hopes up. Anything Taylor told him had to be taken with a healthy dose of skepticism.

Leaning on a walking cane, Skip Taylor, dressed in a thin white T-shirt, pajama bottoms and a white robe, eased down on the opposite side of the bench. Grunting and wincing, he put the cane on the arm of the bench.

"Nice out here, huh?" said Skip. "Nice day. Blue skies. Puffy white clouds. Beautiful island. I could stay here forever. Maybe—"

"Maybe you ought to tell me why you wanted to meet out here," suggested Leo. "I'm not interested in small talk—"

"Derek is telling the truth," said Skip, staring straight ahead. "Aaron Jones was blackmailing him."

"Derek said you would say that," said Leo.

"You think I'm full of shit?" Skip scoffed. "Believe me, or don't. It's up to you, but I'm telling you that Jones was blackmailing Derek. He emailed Derek, hassling him. Derek called me, and I took over. I negotiated with Jones. We go back and forth. I'm trying to find out if this crazy bastard has evidence that will ruin Derek's life, according to him. Because for all I know, he's running a scam, right?"

"Did Jones have evidence against Derek?"

Skip exhaled. "Jones tells me he knows why Derek was fired from Hennessy Capital."

"Why was Derek fired?" asked Leo.

"Last year, sometime around March, if I remember correctly," began Skip, "Derek got into a bit of trouble. Gambling debt. Two million."

Leo gaped at the fixer. "Two million?"

Skip said, "He panics because he can't pay it and he can't go to his father, because Derek made a promise not to gamble after his old man bailed him out several times the previous year. So he calls me for help."

"And how did you help him?"

After a sigh, Skip said, "I suggested that he *borrow* the money from his father's investment firm."

Leo felt his pulse jump. "And by 'borrow', you mean steal, right?"

"Actually," said Skip, stroking his chin. "I believe the term is embezzle."

"Are you serious?"

"Derek didn't know the first thing about how to embezzle funds," said Skip, chuckling. "He's used to having everything handed to him on a platinum platter. So, anyway, I give him step-by-step detailed instructions. In the meantime, I tell him I'll work on negotiating a payment plan with the thugs he owed money to, the Russian mob."

Rubbing his temple, Leo tried to massage away the impending headache.

"Derek follows my instructions and creates fake vendors and bank accounts," said Skip. "He gets everything in place and then he fucks up everything."

"How?"

"Instead of siphoning the money in small amounts, like I told him, which would not have raised any flags," said Skip, "Derek decides to authorize the payment of a two million dollar invoice which sets off loud, clanging alarm bells in the accounting department at Hennessy Capital."

Nodding, Leo said, "Derek wanted to pay off the entire two million as soon as possible."

"Which he was able to do," said Skip. "But, in doing that, he gets the attention of accounting and IT, who request a private emergency meeting with David Hennessy. Long story short, after a very thorough investigation, accounting and IT report to old man Hennessy that the funds were likely embezzled by Derek."

Exhaling, Leo stared toward the man-made lake.

"Old man Hennessy confronts Derek who reluctantly comes clean," said Skip. "David will keep things quiet and take the hit and he won't have Derek arrested, but he fires Derek and kicks him out of the family."

Leo struggled to wrap his mind around what Derek had done. The scope and magnitude of Derek's selfish stupidity astounded Leo. What the hell had Derek been thinking? Embezzling from his family's company? The Hennessy investment empire would have been beyond ruined, and would likely have never recovered from Derek's actions had they been made public. Investors would have fled as the company struggled to withstand withering criminal investigations and massive lawsuits. In the end, Hennessy Capital would have gone down as yet another crooked conglomerate, joining the likes of Enron, WorldCom, and Lehman Brothers.

Shaking his head, Skip said, "I coulda throttled Derek. But, you know who was on his side? Besi. She didn't kick him when he was down. One hundred percent supportive, she was. Derek came clean to her about the embezzlement and you know what she says?"

Leo wasn't sure he wanted to know. "What?"

"Besi tells Derek, next time you get into trouble, you come to me," said Skip. "That girl, bless her heart and God rest her soul, she really loved him. She tells him she's got access to her five hundred million dollar trust and she would have helped him. After that, me and Besi made a pact. Together, we would make sure Derek stayed out of trouble."

"By paying off his gambling debts?" asked Leo. "Maybe instead you should have helped him kick his gambling habit."

Skip shrugged. "You're probably right, but anyway, after Derek got fired, he and Besi got closer, and they fell in love. Derek proposes. They decide to have a fairytale wedding on this gorgeous island. Then, Derek got an email from that asshole, Aaron Jones. Derek panics because Jones claims he knows why Derek was fired from Hennessy Capital and he wants a hundred large."

Leo asked, "How did Jones find out that Derek was fired for embezzling money?"

"I didn't ask." Skip shrugged. "What did it matter how he found out? Problem was that he knew and we had to take care of the situation. Had to pay that piece of shit, which Derek did."

Leo scoffed. "Don't you mean Besi paid Jones for Derek? Isn't that why Besi came to see you before she was killed? You wanted Besi to give you the money to pay off Jones."

Skip shook his head. "Derek said he didn't want Besi bailing him out."

Skeptical, Leo asked, "Where did Derek get the money?"

Shrugging, Skip said, "He had some savings."

Leo supposed that was plausible.

Skip said, "After Derek had the money transferred from his bank account to the Pourciau Bank, the cash was withdrawn, and I gave Jones the hundred thousand dollars."

"Which was stuffed into Derek's Hermes briefcase."

"Wasn't stuffed," said Skip. "The money was bundled in stacks and placed neatly in the briefcase, which Jones liked. Thought it was snazzy. His word, not mine. I told him to keep it. Figured, what the hell."

"The briefcase had Derek's fingerprints on it," said Leo. "Did you know that? That's how the cops put Derek in Jones' motel room."

"That one's on me," said Skip. "But, I thought Jones would take the money and the briefcase and leave the island. Never thought he'd get his ass shot off."

"What do you know about that?" Leo asked.

"About Jones getting shot?" Skip shook his head. "Not a damn thing. Must have been some shit he was mixed up in that didn't have nothing to do with Derek."

"Jones was mixed up in Besi's murder," said Leo, fighting the urge to grab the walking cane and whack Skip Taylor across the head with it. "That has everything to do with Derek."

Skip shook his head. "Jones wasn't involved with Besi's murder."

"The cops believe Jones killed her," said Leo. "The gun used to kill Besi was found in his motel room."

"I don't know how the gun got in his motel room," said Skip. "What I know is Jones ain't the guy who killed Besi. Jones was a blackmailer. He wasn't no hitman. Trust me. I know guys that do wet work. They got a look. A way they carry themselves. Jones didn't have it in him to blow nobody's brains out."

"Well, somebody killed Besi."

"Wasn't Jones," Skip reiterated. "He was looking for a payoff. He wanted to make a deal. Money in exchange for evidence."

"Jones gave you the evidence he had on Derek?"

Skip nodded. "Handed me one of them oversized envelopes. Says, it's all in here. I took it back to the place I'm renting, a little house in a neighborhood called Oyster Farms."

"What was in the envelope?"

"I was expecting a bunch of damaging emails about Derek's crimes between David Hennessy and the company's HR and Legal departments," said Skip, "but wasn't nothing like that."

"What was it?"

"Emails that Jones wrote to himself about Derek's termination, but no proof about the embezzlement that would have incriminated Derek. No documents about *why* Derek had been fired, or nothing like that. It was kinda like Jones' personal email diary, but it could have been easily disputed. Wasn't like he had any Hennessy Capital emails about the situation."

"That doesn't make any sense."

"Wasn't the only thing that didn't make sense," said Skip. "Jones had a separate file with stuff in it about Besi."

"Besi?"

Shaking his head, Skip said, "Crazy, unbelievable stuff. I called her and told her to meet me at the Oyster Farms house I was renting. Said it was very important that we talk about the crazy stuff that Jones gave me."

"What did Besi say about the stuff?" asked Leo.

Skip shrugged. "She never showed up."

Surprised, Leo asked, "She didn't?"

Shaking his head, Skip said, "She said she was coming, but she ghosted me."

"What was in the envelope?" asked Leo, wondering where Besi had gone in the white BMW if she hadn't met with Skip at the Oyster Farms house.

Skip said, "You need to see for yourself or you ain't gonna believe me."

"Where is it?"

"Hid it in the attic at the rental house," said Skip.

Fighting frustration, Leo said, "Give me an idea of what I'm going to find inside."

"Crazy shit regarding Besi," said Skip. "It's gonna be hard to believe, but—"

A gasping grunt escaped the fixer's lips as he leaned forward, and slumped to the ground.

Leo jumped up, gazing at the back of the fixer's head—what was left of it

...

Heart lurching, Leo stared at Skip Taylor's skull, which seemed to have exploded into a pulpy mass of blood, brains, and bone.

33

"Baxter François doesn't believe my story," said Leo, dropping down on the couch against the wall in Vivian's office. "He thinks there's something I'm not telling him."

Stretching out on the plush cushions, Leo closed his eyes and tried to forget about the terse interrogation he'd endured. Three hours of evading and avoiding, trying to make sure he didn't get tripped up by the detective's verbal sleight of hand and cunning misdirection.

Two days had passed since Skip Taylor was shot in the back of the head, in broad daylight, right in front of him. After alerting the hospital staff and calling the police, Leo had dropped to his knees and tried to give the fixer CPR. Seconds later, an emergency response team took over while Leo glanced around the area, scanning the trees and bushes behind the bench where he and Skip had been sitting, trying to determine where the shot had been fired from. When the deputies arrived, Leo gave his statement, revealing only that he was trying to find out if Skip knew anything about Derek's involvement in Besi's murder but the fixer had been shot before Leo could get any information out of him.

"He's right," said Vivian. "There is something you're not telling him. François thinks Derek paid Jones to kill Besi. He has no idea that Jones was blackmailing Derek."

"I can't tell him that," said Leo, opening his eyes. "Not yet. Not until I figure out the truth. Not until I can determine whether or not Derek was being blackmailed."

"Skip Taylor confirmed Derek's story," said Vivian.

"Did he confirm Derek's story because it's true?" asked Leo, staring at the ceiling tiles. "Or, because Derek paid him to confirm his story?"

Vivian sighed. "How do we figure out the truth?"

Leo wished he knew.

What Skip Taylor had confided in him only confused the issue even more. The whole situation was already like a giant puzzle missing several pieces. Skip had provided additional pieces, but Leo couldn't figure out how to make them fit.

"You know what's so weird," said Vivian. "According to Skip, Jones blackmailed Derek by claiming he has proof of why Derek was fired. But, when Jones gave Skip the evidence that could ruin Derek's life, none of it would really hurt Derek. But he does have something on Besi. What's up with that? What could be so crazy about Besi?"

"We need to see what's inside that envelope," said Leo, sitting up and swinging his legs to the floor. "Skip said it was hidden in the attic at the Dove Street house."

"Can't go today," said Vivian. "Sophie says the Dove Street house is still swarming with cops collecting evidence."

Leo cursed.

"Speaking of Sophie," said Vivian. "She's developing a good relationship with Officer Fields. He confided in her that the handprint on the glass pane was blood—which Detective François conveniently avoided telling me when I asked him—and Fields told her the blood was Skip Taylor's."

"I didn't get a chance to ask Skip about the break-in," said Leo.

"According to Sophie," said Vivian, "Fields said the cops' theory is that Skip Taylor surprised a burglar who shot him and then chased Skip into the street where he was accidentally hit by a car."

"Was anything taken from the house?"

"Not that the cops could tell," said Vivian. "But the cops identified Skip a week, or so, ago, when he was hit by the car. He had his wallet with him. They decided not to share that information with the media, however."

"See, the cops keep secrets, too," said Leo.

"Speaking of secrets," said Vivian. "I've been thinking about the reason Derek was fired from Hennessy Capital. I wish Skip had asked Aaron Jones how he found out."

Rubbing his eyes, Leo said, "So do I, but—"

There was a knock on the door.

Leo sat up as Vivian called out, "Come in."

With his customary slow, loitering stride, Stevie Bishop loped into the office, with a lopsided grin and a manila folder.

"Got some results from my cousin," said Stevie, waving the folder.

Smiling, Vivian clapped her hands. "What did your cousin find out?"

"Did he trace the number associated with the anonymous texts Besi received from the mystery burner phone?" asked Leo.

"Yes and the mystery burner wasn't really a burner," said Stevie, dropping down in the chair in front of Vivian's desk. "It was a legit phone registered to Aaron Jones."

"Are you serious?" Vivian asked.

"Why the hell would Besi and Aaron Jones have been in contact with each other?" asked Leo.

Stevie said, "These emails may shed some light on that."

"What emails?" asked Vivian.

"My cousin found some deleted emails on Besi's real phone," said Stevie. "They're very interesting. I printed them out for you."

Stevie handed Vivian a manila file folder.

Opening the file, Vivian removed one of the print-outs and stared at it. "Interesting is an understatement."

"What do the emails say?" asked Leo.

Clearing her throat, Vivian read: "Ms. Beaumont. My name is Aaron Jones. I am a private investigator."

"Jones was a P.I.?" interjected Leo.

Stevie said, "Which makes me think that maybe he was blackmailing Derek Hennessy."

Vivian continued: "Recently, I have learned of disturbing facts that you should know. Please contact me on this secure line: 555-8977."

"The strange burner phone," said Leo.

Nodding, Vivian read, "Time is of the essence. Please do not delay in contacting me as soon as possible. Sincerely, A. Jones."

"What the hell?" Leo shook his head. "What do the other emails say?"

Vivian read the second email. "Ms. Beaumont, two weeks ago, I contacted you regarding disturbing facts that I feel you should be made aware of so that you can deal with these facts swiftly and accordingly. As I have not heard from you, I must implore you to contact me as soon as possible and do not delay. Sincerely, A. Jones."

"What do you want to bet that those 'disturbing facts' had to do with why Derek was fired from Hennessy Capital?" asked Leo. "Jones was a private investigator, so that's probably how he found out about Derek."

"But, why?" asked Stevie.

Leo glanced at Stevie. "Why what?"

"Why did Jones start looking into why Derek was fired?" asked Stevie. "Someone must have hired Jones."

"Maybe it was Elizabeth A. Davis," Leo said.

"Who's Elizabeth A. Davis?" asked Stevie.

"The brunette in the sunglasses," said Leo. "Jones' accomplice, according to the cops."

"Let me read the rest of the emails," suggested Vivian. "Maybe they'll answer our questions. The third email from Aaron says: Ms. Beaumont, apparently, for some reason, you are ignoring me. That would be a mistake. I have information you need to know. If you do not contact me today—and today is typed in all caps—I plan to release the information I know to the public. I hope you make the right decision and contact me immediately! This is your final warning. A. Jones."

Stevie said, "Sounds like Jones was threatening to tell the world why Derek was fired."

Dragging a hand along his jaw, Leo said, "But, the thing is, according to Skip, Besi already knew why Derek had been fired. Jones wasn't going to tell Besi something she wasn't aware of."

"Maybe that's why Besi was ignoring Jones," opined Stevie. "She already knew what he was going to tell her."

Vivian said, "What Besi didn't know was whether or not Jones was serious about revealing what he knew. Obviously, Besi wouldn't want anyone to know why Derek had been fired."

"Why was he fired?" Stevie asked.

"That's not the point," said Leo, wondering why he'd been so quick to keep Derek's secret. The bastard's reputation did not deserve to be protected. "We need to find out who hired Jones to investigate the reason behind Derek's termination. My money is on Elizabeth A. Davis."

Vivian said, "Let's continue with the emails before we start speculating. The fourth email says, Ms. Beaumont, we must meet again concerning an extremely urgent matter! I have come into possession of information that you must be made aware of. This information will be life-changing to you! Please call me immediately! A. Jones."

"Wait a minute," said Stevie. "Read that email again."

After Vivian complied, Stevie said, "Did you guys catch that?"

Frowning at Stevie, Leo asked, "Catch what?"

Stevie said, "Jones wrote 'we must meet again,' which means that after the third email where Jones mentioned Derek, Besi must have decided to meet with him."

"Good catch, Stevie," said Vivian. "I totally missed that."

Grudgingly impressed with Stevie, Leo nodded. "During that meeting, I'm guessing Jones told Besi that he knew why Derek had been fired and he probably outlined his payment demands."

Vivian said, "But, why did they have to meet again? At their first meeting, Jones told Besi the urgent, life-changing information he knew. So, what's with this email about more urgent information that Besi had to know?"

Leo was stumped. "Maybe the urgent, life-changing information had something to do with the crazy stuff about Besi in the file that Jones gave Skip Taylor."

"There's crazy stuff about Besi in a file?" asked Stevie.

"I'll tell you after Vivian reads the last email," said Leo.

"The last email is from Besi to Jones," said Vivian. "And it seems Jones did get Besi's attention because Besi emailed Jones about her plans to visit the Aerie Islands. In this email, she tells Jones to meet her there so they can discuss things further."

34

Finishing an email to the Bronson Publishing Digital Marketing department, Vivian used her mouse to click the send button and then leaned back in her creaky leather chair.

She grabbed the cup of coffee sitting on her desk calendar and took a sip. She could go for a blueberry muffin to complement the strong brew, especially since she'd spent most of the morning talking to Melanie.

Forsaking Lemmie's delightful breakfast buffet, Vivian had asked Melanie about the deleted emails Stevie's hacker cousin had retrieved from Besi's phone. Shocked by the emails, Melanie claimed to have no idea that the man who'd been harassing Besi was Aaron Jones, the person who eventually had killed her.

"Sorry about all the questions," Vivian had said as the conversation wound down. "Thanks for talking to me."

"I'm sorry I couldn't be more helpful," said Melanie. "Guess I didn't know my best friend as well as I thought I did."

Melanie's pronouncement struck a melancholy, depressing chord within Vivian. Instantly, she'd been reminded of how she, too, hadn't known her best friend. She was debating whether or not to admit that she could empathize when Melanie said, "Listen, I want to apologize for my behavior at dinner the other night. I didn't mean to lose it and slap Derek. I was thinking more about the Rolex. I remember asking Besi about the watch when she came back from the Aerie Islands. At first, she didn't seem to know what I was talking about but then she remembered and said she was going to give it to him, but maybe she didn't. Maybe Derek was telling the truth. In any event, I'm truly sorry for making a scene."

Nodding, Vivian said, "No apologies necessary. This situation has been very devastating, and no one blames you for being frustrated. But, I have to ask. Do you really think Derek hired someone to kill Besi?"

Melanie had admitted that she wasn't sure what she believed, and then said, "But, it wasn't right to blame Derek for the surgery. Besi always hated that bump in her nose. Sometimes, she would wear glasses to try and hide it. She always told me that she didn't know where the bump even came from because her father doesn't have a bump in his nose and neither does her mom. Besi always wanted to look like her mom. They could have been twins except Besi had that bump, but her mom didn't."

"Was Besi close to her mother?"

"They were very close," said Melanie. "Besi took it really hard when her mom passed away, especially with her dad having dementia. She felt like she'd lost both of her parents. Would have been easier for her if she had a brother or a sister, but she was an only child. All alone in the world."

Trading the coffee for a red editing pen, Vivian made a few doodles on a legal pad.

Thinking about the revelations from the deleted emails, Vivian recalled the conclusions she, Leo, and Stevie had come to in her office yesterday afternoon.

Aaron Jones, a private investigator, contacted Besi three times about urgent, life-changing information she needed to know and warned her not to ignore him.

Eventually, Besi agreed to meet Jones.

During that meeting, Jones and Besi came to an agreement where Jones would stay quiet about what he knew in exchange for a certain amount of money.

Then, a month later, Jones contacted Besi a fourth time claiming to have more urgent information she needed to know and shouldn't ignore.

Besi agreed to meet Jones in the Aerie Islands, where she was travelling to have plastic surgery in advance of her wedding to Derek

Presumably, Besi and Jones did meet in the Aerie Islands.

While in the Aerie Islands, Besi's purse was stolen and she had the surgery to remove the bump in her nose. Also, while in the Aerie Islands, Besi and Jones exchanged strange texts about a woman named Elizabeth A. Davis who wasn't going to stay quiet.

A week before Besi and Derek's wedding was scheduled, Jones arrived in St. Killian, from the Aerie Islands, with a brunette in sunglasses, recently identified as Elizabeth A. Davis, the woman who wasn't going to stay quiet.

Jones blackmailed Derek with the information about the reason for Derek's termination from Hennessy Capital.

And then, Jones killed Besi …

Vivian thought it all added up to something she should be able to figure out, and yet she couldn't. She wasn't sure if the pieces were all there, but she couldn't make them fit. Or, maybe she knew what the picture should look like, but several pieces were missing. Either way, the puzzle was still unsolved.

There were still too many questions, too many unknowns. She couldn't form any hypothetical theories. What was the additional urgent information that Jones travelled to the Aerie Islands to tell Besi? How had Jones found out about the additional urgent information? Did Elizabeth A. Davis know about that information? Maybe Elizabeth A. Davis had agreed to stay quiet about why Derek had been fired—assuming, as Leo believed, that she had hired Jones to investigate Derek's termination—but she refused to stay quiet about the additional life-changing information? Why? Because she wanted more money and Besi wouldn't give it to her?

Vivian's phone buzzed, breaking into her thoughts, and she pressed the button to answer it. "Yes, Millie."

"There's an Officer Damon Fields here to see Sophie, but she's out on a story," said the receptionist. "You want to talk to him instead?"

"Absolutely," said Vivian. "Send him to my office."

Moments later, Officer Damon Fields, a tall, gangly St. Killian native with a wide, engaging smile took a seat. After a few minutes of entertaining small talk, Vivian invited the officer to tell her why he'd stopped by.

"Got a tip for Sophie," said Officer Fields. "We've been, um, collaborating, off the record, of course—"

"Of course," said Vivian. "And I'm glad you feel comfortable confiding in Sophie. She's a good reporter, and you're a good source, hopefully, one we can count on, in the future, and certainly a source that we'll appreciate and always respect. Anonymous source truly means anonymous. You won't have to worry about us accidentally on purpose attributing a quote to you."

"I appreciate your discretion," said Officer Fields.

"So, tell me about this tip you have."

"Has to do with the Aaron Jones murder," said Officer Fields. "You know about the gun found in Jones' motel room, right?"

"The AR-15 ghost gun used to kill Besi Beaumont."

Officer Fields nodded. "The gun had fingerprints on it."

Vivian nodded. "Detective François told me that."

"We expected to find Aaron Jones' prints on the gun," said Officer Fields. "But, we didn't."

"Whose prints were on the gun?" asked Vivian.

"They belong to a guy named Manny LaRoche," said Officer Fields. "He's a low-rent gun for hire. We picked him up in Handweg yesterday and he had a lot to say about the murder of Bessemer Beaumont."

35

"Aaron Jones didn't kill Besi," announced Vivian, closing the door behind her after entering Leo's office.

"What the hell are you talking about?" asked Leo.

"We've got to get the story out right now," said Vivian, sitting on the edge of her husband's desk. "And we need maximum exposure so I've called a meeting with the online publicity department."

"Wait a minute," said Leo. "If Aaron Jones didn't kill Besi, then who the hell did?"

"Manny LaRoche," said Vivian, and then shared with Leo the bombshell information Fields had given her.

LaRoche, a St. Killian native and wanna-be gangbanger, had received a call from an acquaintance, a man who turned out to be the pilot who'd flown Aaron Jones and Elizabeth A. Davis from the Aerie Islands to St. Killian. The pilot, who also flew drugs and illegal guns for the PC-5, had a job opportunity for LaRoche.

A five thousand dollar job LaRoche wasn't going to pass up, even though he didn't exactly have the skills, or the tools, to carry out a hit, according to Fields. As LaRoche spilled his guts to the St. Killian cops, the wet work entailed kidnapping a woman, killing her, and then disposing of the dead body.

"Are you serious?" Leo shook his head.

Vivian said, "LaRoche identified Aaron Jones as the man who hired him. LaRoche and Jones met at the Flamingo Inn and sealed the deal. LaRoche still had the photo of Besi that Jones had given him. LaRoche was supposed to grab Besi while she was away from the mansion, but he wasn't able to do that because Besi rarely left the mansion."

"Except for that one time when she went to Oyster Farms and then decided not to meet with Skip," said Leo.

"LaRoche got desperate and ended up shooting Besi at her wedding," said Vivian. "Apparently, LaRoche had been staking out the mansion and found out the wedding color scheme. He showed up to kill Besi in a peach blazer and accidentally ripped the blazer in his haste to flee the scene and left behind a piece of fabric in the bushes."

"Which the cops mistakenly thought was fabric from one of the bridesmaid's dresses."

"LaRoche didn't even have a gun," said Vivian, trying to remember all the details Fields had given her. "That's why Jones bought a PC-5 ghost gun."

Leo said, "And paid for it with Derek's Rolex."

"Which makes me wonder …"

"Makes you wonder what?" asked Leo.

"Derek said Besi never gave him that Rolex."

Leo exhaled. "Derek lied."

"But, what if he didn't," suggested Vivian.

"Then how the hell did Jones get that Rolex if Derek didn't give it to him?"

Vivian said, "I don't know, but—"

A sharp, percussive knock interrupted Leo.

"You expecting company?" asked Vivian, heading away from the desk, toward the door.

Leo shook his head. "But, I welcome the interruption."

Opening the door, Vivian stepped back, allowing junior reporters Stevie Bishop and Sophie Carter to enter Leo's office. "Look, Leo, it's our dynamic duo."

Groaning, Leo said, "Hmmm, babe, I think we're about to be double-teamed."

Laughing, Vivian invited Stevie and Sophie to take the seats in front of Leo's desk.

"We heard there's a huge break in the Besi Beaumont murder case," said Stevie.

"Where did you hear that?" asked Leo.

"I ran into Officer Fields as he was leaving," said Sophie, glancing at Vivian. "He told me he'd passed on some information to you that he wanted me to know and when I pressed him, he told me that Aaron Jones didn't kill Besi."

Vivian nodded. "That's true. Maybe you should write the story?"

Sophie's eyes lit up as an infectious smile spread across her face. "Are you serious?"

Stevie said, "Sophie was hoping you would say that."

Frowning at Stevie, Sophie gave him a light punch on his arm. "I was not."

"You were, too," countered Stevie.

As Leo rubbed his eyes, Vivian caught his look of irritation. Worried, she walked behind her husband's chair and placed her hands on his shoulders.

"I was not," insisted Sophie.

Stevie said. "You were—"

"Sophie, I want the *Palmchat Gazette* to be the first to break the story about Manny LaRoche," said Vivian, hoping her gentle massage would temper Leo's frustrations. "So, you should get on it."

Solemn and serious, Sophie nodded and then turned to Stevie. "Can you tell Viv and Leo about Elizabeth A. Davis?"

As Sophie rushed out of the office, Leo asked, "What about Elizabeth A. Davis?"

"My cousin found an email on Jones' phone, formerly known as the mystery burner phone found in Besi's luggage, and in that email, Elizabeth A. Davis asks Aaron Jones to call her and she gives him her phone number," said Stevie, plopping down in one of the chairs in front of Leo's desk. "So, me and Sophie used that phone number to trace Elizabeth A. Davis, who is from Los Angeles, California."

"And?" prompted Leo.

"And up until his death last year, she lived with her late father …

Guillermo Davis." "Samuel Beaumont's former chauffeur," said Vivian, remembering the information Sophie had emailed her. "He was rumored to have had an affair with Besi's mother, Adrienne."

"I wonder if Besi knew Elizabeth Davis," said Leo, leaning forward, away from Vivian's touch.

"They might have been friends," said Vivian.

"Possibly," said Stevie. "Elizabeth A. Davis is about a year and some months older than Besi."

"I wonder if maybe Besi confided in Elizabeth A. Davis about Derek's embezzling," said Vivian.

Leo said, "And Elizabeth A. Davis told Aaron Jones and then Elizabeth and Jones decided to blackmail Besi, who would not have wanted Derek's embezzling to come out because she wouldn't want her fiancé to go to jail."

"Sounds probable," said Stevie.

Vivian asked, "But, then how did Jones and Besi get to the point where they were texting about Elizabeth not staying quiet?"

"Here's how I see it," said Leo. "Let's say Besi knows Elizabeth Davis because of the history between Besi's mom and Elizabeth's dad. Somehow, they become friends. Besi tells Elizabeth why Derek was fired from Hennessy Capital and Elizabeth decides to use that information to her advantage. She calls her buddy Jones and has him contact Besi, thus leaving her out of it and that's how I think things went sideways."

"I don't understand," said Stevie.

Vivian did, however. "Jones must have tried to cut Elizabeth A. Davis out of the deal with Besi. So, Elizabeth decided to ruin everything by threatening to spill the tea about Derek's termination, and if she had, if she wouldn't stay quiet, then Besi would have no reason to pay Jones."

"But, Besi would still try to stop Elizabeth from ratting about Derek," said Leo. "So, she wants Jones to help her deal with Elizabeth. Maybe that's why Jones and Besi met in the Aerie Islands. To come up with a plan to make sure Elizabeth stayed quiet. I'm thinking when Jones and Besi met the first time, they agreed on payment terms and thought everything was settled. But, then maybe Elizabeth and Jones had a falling out over the money and Elizabeth threatened to renege on the agreement."

"So, Jones sends that fourth email about the additional urgent information," said Vivian. "He was talking about Elizabeth threatening to blow up the deal."

Stevie nodded. "Makes sense."

"Then why do I have a feeling there's something we're missing," said Leo.

Vivian said, "You mean, how things get to the point where Jones ended up blackmailing Derek and then hiring a hitman to kill Besi?"

"Exactly," said Leo. "That's what we don't know and that's why we need to find Elizabeth A. Davis. Besi is dead and so is Jones. Elizabeth is the only one still alive who can answer those questions."

36

At five o'clock on a blustery, balmy afternoon, Vivian could think of a dozen other things she would rather be doing than trespassing at the Dove Street house in Oyster Farms, but Leo had insisted. She wasn't going to let Leo go alone, even though she didn't agree with the idea.

Her husband was convinced that there was a piece of the puzzle they needed to find, the crucial piece, the piece that would enable them to finally see the whole picture. Leo was certain they would find that puzzle piece in the envelope Skip Taylor had hidden in the attic at the house on Dove Street.

And now, after they'd headed into the backyard and slipped under the yellow crime scene tape, they stood in the kitchen of the rental home, staring at the envelope Leo had retrieved from the attic moments ago.

"You think we'll find the missing piece to the puzzle in here?" asked Vivian as she opened the envelope and pulled out a blue file stuffed with papers. Removing the documents, she placed them in a stack on the table.

Leo exhaled and rubbed his jaw. "I'm a little concerned about what we're going to find. Part of me wants the answers, but if we get them, then what? And if we don't, then …"

Vivian looked left, glancing at the shattered patio door they'd entered.

Late afternoon sunlight crept through the house, casting a coppery glow into the living area that spread into the kitchen.

Exhaling, she picked up the first few documents. "These seem to be ... articles about Hennessy Capital. Articles about David Hennessy and Derek ... just seems like a bunch of research about the Hennessy family. Doesn't seem to be anything about Derek's embezzlement or his termination."

Leo grabbed the next document. "This is an email from Aaron Jones to Aaron Jones. Skip Taylor mentioned something about Aaron Jones writing emails to himself."

Taking the email from her husband, Vivian read: "Recently, I was made aware of the following facts which I cannot independently confirm but which were told to me by a highly credible and reliable source with intimate details of this matter, which are as follows: Last year, on or around March, Derek Hennessy willfully embezzled funds in the amount of two million dollars from Hennessy Capital, a leading investment firm with assets in the billions which is founded/owned by David Hennessy, Derek's father. Derek Hennessy was employed at Hennessy Capital until he was terminated for embezzling the funds from his father's company."

"No wonder Skip Taylor decided to pay Jones," said Leo.

"But who is this reliable, credible source with intimate knowledge of the matter?" asked Vivian. "Elizabeth A. Davis, maybe?"

Leo said, "Maybe it was Skip Taylor."

"You think Skip told Jones why Derek was fired?" Vivian grabbed another document. "Skip didn't even know Jones."

Sighing, Leo said, "I'm not sure what to think but there weren't too many people with intimate knowledge of the matter who could have told Jones besides Skip, Besi, David Hennessy and Derek himself. Of those four, my money would be on Skip."

"I still think Elizabeth A. Davis told Jones," said Vivian.

Leo said, "Speaking of Elizabeth, here's an email she sent to Jones in January of this year. The one Stevie told us about. Elizabeth writes to Aaron: Hey, it's Lizzie. I need you to look into something for me. Call me. And she gives her number. Wonder what Elizabeth wanted Jones to look into?"

"Whatever it was, Elizabeth was anxious to get answers," said Vivian, skimming the next series of documents, which were all emails between Elizabeth A. Davis and Aaron Jones. "Jones must have agreed to help her because she sent an email asking him if he had any news for her. Jones replied that he was still working on it."

Leo said, "Apparently, Jones got answers because he wrote in an email to Elizabeth that he had news and wanted to meet her to discuss it."

"Jones' news had something to do with Besi," said Vivian, staring at the next email. "In April, Jones wrote to Elizabeth: Spoke to Bessemer Beaumont. She has agreed to your terms and will meet with us this month in the Aerie Islands. Elizabeth replies that she wants to meet with Jones to discuss the details."

"The fact that Besi agreed to Elizabeth's term means we were right about Elizabeth blackmailing Besi," said Leo.

Vivian said, "We were thinking that Elizabeth was threatening to expose Derek's embezzlement, which Elizabeth knew about because Besi had confided in her, however …"

"The emails between Elizabeth and Jones suggest that Elizabeth wanted him to investigate something for her."

"Something about Besi that Jones must have confirmed," said Vivian. "Something that could be used to blackmail Besi."

"Elizabeth could blackmail Besi with the truth about Derek's termination," said Leo. "Maybe Elizabeth wanted Jones to investigate why Derek had been fired from Hennessy Capital because she suspected he'd done something criminal."

"That's what I'd thought," said Vivian, "but Jones emailed himself in July saying he'd found out that Derek had embezzled money from Hennessy Capital. If Elizabeth wanted Jones to look into the reason for Derek's termination, then according to the emails between Jones and Elizabeth, Jones discovered the reason in March."

Leo nodded. "Then why, in July, would Jones say that he'd recently found out about Derek embezzling? So, we're back to the question—what did Elizabeth want Jones to investigate?"

"I don't know, but there are no more emails," said Vivian, walking from the table to the center island. "This next document is a letter to Elizabeth A.

Davis. It starts: 'Hello Elizabeth Adrienne, my name is Adrienne Elizabeth—"

"Adrienne Elizabeth?" asked Leo, walking toward the island. "Why would Besi's mother be writing a letter to Elizabeth Davis?"

"Let me keep reading and find out," said Vivian. "My name is Adrienne Elizabeth. This is the hardest letter I have ever had to write. I wish I did not have to write it. I wish I could tell you these things in person, but I am afraid that I am not well at the moment and unable to travel. Due to my illness, which I am, unfortunately, not expected to survive, I fear I will never get the chance to see you in person, which breaks my heart."

"Besi's mom died of cancer," said Leo.

"But, I have something very important to tell you," read Vivian. "Something I should have told you long ago, and I would have if I were not selfish."

Leo shook his head. "What could Besi's mom have to tell Elizabeth Davis? Babe, can you skip to the end?"

Walking around the island, Vivian stood in front of the sink and skimmed the words, written in a precise, controlled, cursive. As she read the words from Besi's mother to Elizabeth Davis, Vivian's heart slammed. Her mind spinning with confusion, she glanced up, staring out of the window above the sink.

"Babe, what is it?" Leo asked.

Taking a deep breath, Vivian turned. On the opposite side of the island, Leo stared at her, confusion in his blue eyes.

"You're not going to believe this," said Vivian. "Adrienne Elizabeth Beaumont is Elizabeth A. Davis' mother."

37

"That can't be right," said Leo, walking around the island toward Vivian. "Besi's an only child. No brothers. No sisters."

"No brothers or sisters that Besi knew about," said Vivian. "But, in this letter, Adrienne Beaumont admits that she kept Elizabeth's existence a secret. Adrienne confesses to Elizabeth that she has a sister named Bessemer, and—"

"Let me see that," said Leo, his pulse skyrocketing as his wife passed the letter to him.

"Adrienne talks about Besi near the end of the letter," said Vivian.

Forcing himself to focus, Leo found the paragraph. "This is crazy. Besi and Elizabeth Davis are sisters? How?"

"Adrienne Beaumont says she had to give Elizabeth up and she regrets it," said Vivian.

"But I want you to know, my sweet Lizzie, that I never stopped thinking about you and I have always loved you as you were my first born child," Leo read. "I wish I could have raised you, but I had no choice but to allow you to be brought up by someone very dear to my heart, a man I knew who would treat you as though you were his own daughter. I know it will come as a shock to you to learn that Guillermo Davis is not your father. What the hell?"

"Let's see what other surprises Jones has," suggested Vivian, grabbing the folder from the island.

"Skip was right," said Leo. "This is crazy shit."

"Damn." Vivian exhaled, shaking her head. "Another letter, but I have no idea what it says. It's written in French. I have no idea what it says."

Shocked, Leo tilted his head, staring at the love of his life. "Babe ... *As-tu oublié que je sais parler français?*"

Eyes wide, Vivian smacked her palm against her forehead. "What was I thinking? Of course, you *parlais Francais.*"

"Trade you," said Leo, handing Vivian the letter from Adrienne to Elizabeth. After taking the letter written in French, he skimmed the first few paragraphs. "This is from Guillermo to Adrienne. It starts my dearest Adrienne, I hope this letter finds you well. I know we have not been able to speak in person, for some time, so I wanted to write to you. He goes on to talk about how Elizabeth is doing well and how she's growing into a beautiful young woman who looks exactly like her mother."

"That's interesting," said Vivian. "I was just wondering if Elizabeth looked anything like Besi and apparently, she looks like her mother, and so did Besi. So, Besi and Elizabeth must resemble each other."

"Wonder if Elizabeth has the bump in her nose," said Leo.

"What else does Guillermo's letter say?"

Leo skimmed the next few paragraphs. "He talks about how he doesn't think it's fair to Elizabeth that she doesn't know her real father. He says ..."

"He says what?"

Clearing his throat, not quite able to believe what he'd read, Leo translated: "Adrienne, I know you think that Lizzie's father is one of the men you were with when you and Sam were having problems in your marriage, but have you considered that maybe Lizzie is Sam's daughter after all?"

Vivian asked, "Could that be true?"

"Guillermo Davis thought so," said Leo, staring at the letter. "He encourages Adrienne to get a DNA test to find out the truth. I wonder if she did it. This letter is dated ten years ago when Elizabeth was sixteen or seventeen years old."

"I think she did," said Vivian. "There's a copy of a DNA test in this folder. But, it looks like the test was done earlier this year, in March."

"And?" Leo asked, his heart starting to pound.

"And Guillermo Davis was right," said Vivian. "Elizabeth Davis is Samuel Beaumont's daughter."

"Babe, what if Elizabeth found this letter from Guillermo Davis to Adrienne where he suggests that Elizabeth is Sam Beaumont's daughter? Elizabeth probably wanted to find out if that was true, so she contacted Aaron Jones to investigate those claims for her."

Vivian nodded. "After Jones confirmed that Samuel was Elizabeth's father, he contacted Besi with this urgent news that she has a sister and ... wait a minute, something's weird. There's a second DNA test in the folder."

"Does the second test dispute the results of the first test?"

Vivian shook her head. "Now I know why Skip said there was crazy shit about Besi in this envelope. Take a look at this."

38

Leo stared at the DNA test, his gaze drawn to the conclusion at the bottom.

He'd already read it several times since Vivian had shown it to him, but he still couldn't believe it, still couldn't understand how the results could be true.

*Conclusion: Samuel Jefferson Beaumont is **excluded** from being the biological father of Bessemer Elizabeth Beaumont. The exclusion is based on the fact that he does not show the genetic markers which have to be present for the biological father of the child, Bessemer Elizabeth Beaumont, at multiple DNA-Systems. Therefore, it is practically proven that Samuel Jefferson Beaumont is **NOT** the biological father of Bessemer Elizabeth Beaumont.*

"Besi wasn't Samuel Beaumont's daughter," said Vivian as she grabbed the folder from the island and tucked the second DNA test inside. "Do you think he knows?"

Facing the window above the sink, Leo shook his head. "Samuel Beaumont is suffering from dementia. Has been for the last five years, or so. He doesn't know one minute from the next."

"You think Elizabeth Davis knows?" asked Vivian. "Has she seen these DNA tests?"

"I don't think so," said Leo. "If Elizabeth knew that she was Sam

Beaumont's daughter, she would have contacted him. She would have wanted to meet her father. And get her share of the Beaumont billions."

"So, maybe Elizabeth didn't know," said Vivian.

"Obviously, Jones knew she was Sam Beaumont's daughter," said Leo. "But, maybe he didn't tell Elizabeth."

"Jones also knew that Besi *wasn't* Sam's daughter," said Vivian. "Where did Jones get copies of the DNA tests? Or, did he have the DNA tests done? And if so, how did he get Besi's DNA? How did he get Sam Beaumont's DNA?"

Leo said, "There's no telling how he got Sam's and Besi's DNA. But, my guess is that Aaron Jones found the letter from Guillermo Davis to Adrienne. He had it translated from French to English, and decided to find out if Sam Beaumont was Elizabeth's father. After confirming that Guillermo was right, Jones might have, for whatever reason, decided to test Besi's DNA and Sam's DNA."

Vivian nodded. "Once Jones learned that Sam wasn't Besi's dad, he probably used those DNA results to blackmail Besi."

Leo said, "Besi would never want the world to know that she wasn't Sam Beaumont's daughter. She adores her father. Worships the ground he walks on. Finding out that Sam wasn't her dad probably damn near killed Besi."

"So, she paid Jones to keep his mouth shut," said Vivian. "Which he does."

"But, somehow, Elizabeth Davis must have found out that Sam Beaumont was her father," said Leo. "She must have threatened to go public."

"That explains the texts about Elizabeth not staying quiet," said Vivian. "But, wait, let's back up. Elizabeth wanted Jones to investigate something for her, remember?"

"Maybe the letter from Guillermo to Adrienne," said Leo. "Elizabeth might have found the letter, and given it to Jones, and asked him to authenticate it, which Jones did, but he didn't tell her."

Vivian sighed. "Because it was explosive information and Jones must have thought he could get more money by blackmailing Besi than coming clean to Elizabeth."

"Doesn't explain the email where Jones tells Elizabeth that Besi agreed to her terms," said Leo. "Unless Besi agreed to acknowledge Elizabeth as Sam's daughter, which I doubt. Why would they meet in the Aerie Islands to do that?"

"And what were Elizabeth's terms that Besi agreed to?" asked Vivian, clutching the folder against her chest as she faced the window.

"But, then, what happened to make Elizabeth threaten to blow up the deal?"

"Elizabeth was causing the problems," said Leo, "and yet Besi ended up dead. You would think that Besi and Jones would have conspired to kill Elizabeth, but—"

The window above the kitchen sink exploded, spewing a hail of glass chunks and shards.

39

Vivian screamed as Leo grabbed her and pulled her to the floor with him, in the space between the island and the sink.

Seconds later, as Vivian tried to think, to figure out what the hell was going on, there was another gunshot. Vivian jumped as Leo pulled her closer, motioning for her to stay quiet. Pressing her lips together, Vivian tried to contain the screams churning in her gut, desperate to be released. Shaking, she pressed the folder against her chest and tried to breathe.

Leo's hand landed on her cheek, and he turned her face toward him.

Staring into his blue eyes, Vivian felt an immediate calmness wash over her, and somehow, she knew everything would be okay. She knew that she and Leo would escape this situation, whatever it was, as they had so many times before.

The concerned determination in Leo's gaze stirred within her a resolute tenacity. Despite the terror running through her veins, Vivian told herself not to panic. Not yet, anyway. Not until they figured out what was happening. All she knew for sure was that someone was in the house. But, why? Had someone seen them sneak inside and follow them? The cops? No, the police would have announced themselves. Maybe a neighbor watching the house for intruders? Or, maybe—

Footsteps came closer.

Vivian froze, listening.

Someone was walking along the opposite side of the island.

Leo motioned for Vivian to follow him as he moved to his hands and knees and headed toward the far end of the island. Her heart slamming, Vivian crawled behind her husband. Leo peeked around the corner of the island, and then looked back at her.

He motioned the direction he wanted them to go, which was straight ahead, into the living area, and beyond that, the shattered patio door. Vivian wasn't great at judging distance, but she guessed they would have to run at least ten feet.

Could they make it without being shot to death?

Vivian wasn't sure and didn't want to chance it. Shaking her head, she beckoned for him to turn and crawl back toward her.

"What is it?" Leo whispered, inches away.

"We need to find out who's in here."

"We need to get the hell out of here," Leo countered. "Then we'll call the cops, and they can find out."

"What if it's a neighbor who was watching the house?" Vivian asked. "If we identify ourselves and—"

A third gunshot rattled Vivian, and she gasped.

"Babe, we have to get out of here," Leo insisted.

Realizing that her husband was right, Vivian nodded.

"On three, okay?" Leo grabbed her hand and rose to his heels. "One, two …"

The three-count came before Vivian was ready, but she managed to stay low, ducking as she ran behind Leo, one hand gripping her husband's, the other clutching the folder.

More bullets rang out as they dashed toward the living area.

"Stop!" A voice cried out, somewhere behind them. "Don't make me kill you!"

Vivian shrieked as Leo grabbed her around the waist, and then vaulted over the sectional sofa, taking her with him. Together, they rolled over the plush cushions and down to the floor, lodged in the space between the couch and the coffee table. As Vivian stared at the ceiling, panting and trying to catch her breath, Leo scrambled on top of her, shielding her with his body.

"Get the hell up. Now!"

Vivian didn't recognize the voice, female but stripped of soft femininity, full of contempt and with a slight Southern drawl. But, from Leo's expression, she could tell her husband knew exactly who was barking orders.

"I don't want to kill you, Leo!"

"I'm getting up," said Leo. "Don't shoot."

"No, please, don't," Vivian whispered, tears rolling down the sides of her face as she wrapped her arms tightly around his waist.

"I'll be okay," he said, pressing his mouth against hers. "I promise."

Squeezing her eyes shut, Vivian shook her head, but she released her hold, allowing him to move away from her. As slowly as possible, Leo rose to his knees and then to his feet.

"Put your hands up where I can see them! No sudden moves or I will shoot, and I promise you, I won't miss!"

Hands raised shoulder high, Leo turned.

"Wow, Leo, you look like you've seen a ghost."

Shaking his head, Leo said, "I don't understand—"

"You don't understand what? How I'm still alive?"

40

"This doesn't make any sense," said Leo.

Unwilling, and unable, to cower in fear, Vivian rolled over onto her stomach and propped herself up on her elbows. Forcing herself to focus, she slipped a shaking hand into the pocket of her blazer and pulled out her cell phone. Fingers trembling, she typed a group text message to the *Palmchat Gazette* staff: *Send police to Dove St. in Oyster Farms!!! ASAP!!!! Leo and I being held at gunpoint! Call cops NOW!!!*

"It makes perfect sense," said Besi.

"We all saw you die," said Leo. "You were shot."

Praying that someone from her staff would call the cops, Vivian put the phone back into her pocket and rose to her feet. Struggling to control her shock and disbelief, she took a deep breath as she stared at the woman standing on the opposite side of the couch.

Leo was right.

It didn't make sense.

Bessemer Beaumont, alive and pointing a gun at them, was beyond impossible.

"No, I wasn't shot," said Besi. "That was my half-sister. Elizabeth Adrienne Davis, who I'm sure you read all about in that file Aaron Jones gave to Skip Taylor."

Vivian opened her mouth but said nothing.

She had no words.

"Speaking of which," said Besi. "Hand over the file. As I said, I don't want to shoot you, but I will if I have to and my daddy taught me how not to miss."

"Your daddy didn't teach you to shoot," said Vivian. "Samuel Beaumont taught you, but he isn't your father."

"I don't care what those DNA tests say," said Besi. "Samuel Beaumont is my father."

"He's Elizabeth Davis' father," Leo said.

Glaring at them, Besi said, "His blood may not run through my veins, but he is the only father that I have ever known and I am the only daughter he raised. Nothing and no one will change that."

"What will he think when he finds out that you're not really his child?" Vivian asked. "And that you killed his daughter?"

"I never thought I would be thankful that my father has dementia," said Besi. "But, thank God, he is completely unaware of reality, and he'll never know—"

"The truth?" interjected Leo.

"He'll never know that his biological daughter kidnapped me and tried to take over my life."

"Tried to take over your life?" Leo asked. "What are you talking about?"

"How did Elizabeth take over your life?" Vivian asked.

Besi rolled her eyes. "You two are investigative journalists, and yet it doesn't seem to have occurred to you that when Elizabeth was killed, she was standing at the altar, making vows to my fiancé. She was pretending to be me. That's why when she was shot, you thought I'd died."

"Explain that to us," said Leo. "How did she end up taking your place?"

"It's a long story," said Besi.

"Isn't it always," said Leo. "Nevertheless, I'd like to hear it."

"Earlier this year," started Besi. "Aaron Jones emailed me about some disturbing facts I needed to know, and he warned me not to ignore him."

"But, you did ignore him," said Vivian, recalling what Melanie had told her about the man who'd been harassing Besi via email.

"The first two times Jones emailed me," said Besi. "I didn't pay him no mind, but when he sent that third email, I got nervous. I started to worry that it had something to do with Derek."

"You thought Jones was one of Derek's bookies?" asked Leo.

Besi nodded. "Derek had gotten into trouble and had to embezzle money from his daddy's company. I didn't want him to do anything foolish again. I didn't want him to risk his freedom or his life. So, I was willing to pay whatever debt he had. Imagine my surprise when Jones tells me he wants to talk about my mama."

"What did Jones have to say about Adrienne?" Leo asked.

"Ridiculous nonsense I refused to believe," said Besi. "Jones told me he was a private investigator and he'd been hired by a woman named Elizabeth A. Davis to find out whether or not she and I were half-sisters. Jones asked me if I would consent to giving some of my DNA to determine if, in fact, me and Elizabeth were related."

"And did you agree?"

"Hell, no," scoffed Besi. "After I refused to take a DNA test, Jones pulls out this letter he claims Mama wrote to Elizabeth—some kind of death bed confession saying she was Elizabeth's mother. He even showed me the letter."

"And you still didn't believe him?"

"Looked like mama's handwriting but some people are good at that sort of thing—forging other people's handwriting."

"How? Would Jones have gotten a copy of Adrienne's handwriting."

"Jones told me Elizabeth had been raised by Guillermo Davis—my daddy's former chauffeur," said Besi. "I'd heard mama and Guillermo were close and mama liked to write letters so I figured she'd probably written to Guillermo. Jones and Elizabeth could have forged mama's handwriting using a letter mama wrote to Guillermo."

Leo said, "But, the letter Adrienne wrote to Guillermo was real."

Besi exhaled. "Yeah, I found that out when Jones claimed he had proof that Elizabeth and I were sisters."

"How'd he get the proof?" asked Leo.

"The sonofabitch stole the cup I'd drank from at the restaurant we met at," said Besi. "He used it to get my DNA and compared it to Elizabeth's

DNA. He was looking for a sibling relationship. The results showed Elizabeth and I shared a common parent—mama."

"Go on," prodded Leo, when Besi's gaze drifted away ... but not too far that she wouldn't be able to get the jump on him if he tried to rush her and grab the gun.

Besi shook her head. "A few weeks after our first meeting, Jones called me. Said he wanted to share some interesting DNA results with me, so I agreed to meet him again. At our second meeting, he explained how he'd stolen my DNA. I was pissed, but DNA don't lie. Jones had exposed my mama's dirty little secrets. Come to find out, a year before I was born, mama gave birth to another baby girl she named Elizabeth. Mama thought one of her many hookups was Elizabeth's father so she sent her off to live with daddy's driver, Guillermo Davis."

"So, you find out you really do have a half-sister," said Leo. "Then what happened?"

Scoffing, Besi said, "Jones said Elizabeth wanted her share of Mama's estate, which she felt she was entitled to because she was Mama's daughter, too. Well, I informed Jones that Mama didn't have any money. That's why she married daddy."

"What did Jones say?" asked Leo.

Besi shrugged. "Wasn't much he could say. I told him to go to hell and to never contact me again."

"But, Jones did contact you again," said Leo.

"He sent me an email claiming he had urgent, life-changing information I had to know and couldn't ignore," said Besi. "I met with him a third time. Turns out it wasn't the charm."

"That's when you found out that Sam Beaumont wasn't your father," said Vivian.

"I'm the bastard daughter who has no idea who her real daddy is," said Besi, an edge to her tone. "I'm the result of mama's skanky sexual shenanigans."

"How did Jones find out that Sam wasn't your father?" asked Leo.

"After our second meeting didn't go as well as Jones had hoped," said Besi, "he and Elizabeth decided to see how much they could get for this locket Mama had mentioned in the letter she wrote to Elizabeth."

"I remember that locket," said Leo, recalling that Tom York had referred to it as a cheap trinket.

"Jones and Elizabeth went looking in Guillermo's attic for the locket, which they found," said Besi. "They'd hoped the locket might be worth some money, but it wasn't even real gold. Jones also found a box of documents and books in the attic that belonged to Guillermo. Jones asked Elizabeth if he could go through the box. He was hoping to find an old insurance policy or some stock certificates that Mama might have left to Elizabeth."

"Jones was determined to benefit from his investigative endeavors," said Leo.

Besi nodded. "Turns out, he did. Or, rather, he would have, if not for Elizabeth."

"He found the letter from Guillermo to Adrienne in that box," Leo said.

"Jones translated it and realized Guillermo suspected that Samuel Beaumont was Elizabeth's daddy," said Besi.

Leo asked, "Did Jones tell Elizabeth what he'd found?"

Besi shook her head. "Jones told me he wanted to verify Guillermo's suspicions before telling Elizabeth."

"How was he able to do that?" asked Vivian.

Besi said, "He went to daddy's estate and bribed one of daddy's nurses to swab the inside of daddy's cheek. Jones did the DNA tests—"

"And proved that Elizabeth's parents were Adrienne and Samuel Beaumont," said Vivian.

"But that got Jones to thinking: Elizabeth's DNA and my DNA showed one common parent, who he assumed to be mama. But if Elizabeth and me have the same mama, then we don't have the same daddy. And if Elizabeth's daddy is Sam Beaumont—"

"Then ... who's your daddy?" asked Leo.

Besi glared at him. "My daddy is Samuel Jefferson Beaumont."

"Not according to the DNA test Jones did on you and Sam Beaumont," said Vivian.

"Jones had no right to test DNA he stole from me against DNA he stole from my daddy," said Besi.

"So Jones tells you that Sam's not your father, and then what?"

"I had a DNA test done to make sure Jones wasn't trying to pull a scam," said Besi. "When I had proof that Jones hadn't lied about Samuel Beaumont not being my daddy, I called him and we met again. I told Jones that if he would tell Elizabeth that Adrienne was her mama, but not mention anything to her about Samuel being her daddy, then I would give him five million dollars. And I told him to tell Elizabeth that I would give her ten million to keep her mouth shut about the fact that she was Adrienne Beaumont's daughter."

Amazed by Jones' duplicity, Vivian asked, "And he agreed?"

"For five million?" Besi scoffed. "You bet your ass he agreed. He took the deal and didn't say anything to Elizabeth about Sam Beaumont being her father. Jones kept his word. But, Elizabeth didn't keep hers ..."

41

"How did Elizabeth not keep her word?"

"Jones convinced Elizabeth to take the ten million dollar deal," said Besi. "He told her I'd changed my mind and was giving her the money so she would stay quiet about being Mama's daughter. But, Elizabeth had another condition—she wanted to meet me in person. Looking back on it now, I never should have agreed to her demand. I should have known she was planning something."

"You agreed to meet Jones and Elizabeth in the Aerie Islands," said Leo.

"I was going to the Rakestraw-Blake Center to get this damn bump removed from my nose," said Besi. "Something I should have done years ago. I figured it would be best to meet at my place down there, so she agreed."

Staring at Besi, Vivian felt something near her hip vibrate. The cell phone. She prayed the message was confirming that the police had been called and were on the way. She hoped her staff didn't think it was a prank or ruse.

"When Elizabeth and I met, it was like looking in a mirror," said Besi, traces of amazement in her tone. "Turns out, we both look exactly like mama—except I had the bump. Elizabeth didn't, but she knew I was getting it removed. And that's when I think Elizabeth decided to get rid of me and steal my life. She never had the bump, so she could pass herself off as me after the plastic surgery."

"So, you meet your half-sister, you look alike, she decides to steal your life and then what?" asked Leo.

"She sent me a text, pretending to be Jones, saying that Elizabeth wasn't going to keep quiet," said Besi. "The fake text from Jones said that he wanted to meet with me, so I agreed to that. When I opened the door, Elizabeth was standing there. She knocked me out. Next thing I know, I'm waking up in the underground hurricane bunker. Aaron Jones is there with me. He's got bad news. He tells me Elizabeth tricked him and forced him, at gunpoint, into the bunker. Apparently, I was out for two or three days. Jones and I figured out that Elizabeth had decided to become Bessemer Beaumont."

"How did the two of you figure out how to get out of the bunker?" asked Vivian.

"Took us about two months, but we found an emergency exit," said Besi.

"How did you survive for two months in a bunker?" asked Leo.

"It's a luxury bunker," said Besi, shrugging. "It's designed to withstand a Cat-5 hurricane. There are about six months' worth of provisions down there. It's got five bedrooms. Five baths. An industrial kitchen. Air conditioning. Bunker cost more than the damn house. Only thing we didn't have was access to outside communication, thanks to Elizabeth. She took our personal phones and the bunker's satellite phones."

"I guess you and Jones got to know each other better," said Leo. "Is that when you came up with a plan to kill Elizabeth."

"Elizabeth didn't give us much of a choice," said Besi. "We doubted she would give up being Bessemer Beaumont. And it wasn't like I could expose what she'd done. Couldn't tell the world that Elizabeth was pretending to be me. She would have denied my claims and in order to prove my identity, both of us would have been forced to do a DNA test to determine which one of us was really the Beaumont heiress."

"If Elizabeth took a DNA test," said Leo. "It would prove that she was the daughter of Samuel and Adrienne Beaumont, not you."

Besi said, "Jones and I realized we had to get rid of Elizabeth."

"So how was it supposed to go?" asked Leo. "Jones hires a guy to kill

Elizabeth, and then you do what? Come back from the dead with some bullshit story about a secret half-sister who tried to steal your life?"

"The plan was that Jones would hire a guy to get rid of Elizabeth before she walked down the aisle," said Besi. "The hitman was supposed to kill her and get rid of the body without anyone ever knowing what he'd done. Ideally, he would have grabbed Elizabeth taking a walk alone on the beach or in her room taking a shower, but he was never able to get her by herself."

"And then with Elizabeth dead and gone, you would have just stepped back into your life with no one the wiser," said Vivian, worrying about the text she'd sent the staff. Had Sophie or Stevie or Beanie taken her message seriously? Had they called the police? Was Baxter François on his way?

"Except you still have the bump," said Leo. "You didn't get the surgery."

"Because my sister knocked me out and stashed me in a bunker," said Besi.

"When people saw you with the bump they would suspect something," said Leo.

"I knew I would have to fake some sort of complication that would send me back to the Rakestraw-Blake Center," said Besi. "I was going to tell everyone that I had to have another surgery but I would actually be getting the bump removed. The wedding date would have to be rescheduled but Derek would have been okay with that."

"How did the plan go sideways?" asked Leo. "How did Jones end up dead?"

42

"Aaron Jones was impatient," said Besi. "And mistrustful. I thought we were on the same page when we left the Aerie Islands, but—"

"You were the brunette in sunglasses who arrived in St. Killian with Jones on that chartered plane?" asked Vivian.

"I had to give away a very expensive piece of jewelry to pay for that flight," said Besi. "But, we couldn't fly commercial, for obvious reasons."

"And that was you at the cocktail party," Vivian said. "Asking about Besi and Derek."

"I bought a brunette wig so no one would notice me," said Besi. "I was hoping to corner Elizabeth so the hitman could kill her, but she'd faked a headache."

"How did you and Jones get off the same page?" Leo asked.

"Elizabeth had taken all of my identification and anything I could use to prove that I was really Bessemer Beaumont," said Besi. "I told Jones money would be tight until I could get my life back. He told me we would need cash to fly to St. Killian and to pay someone to kill Elizabeth."

"How'd you get the money for the hitman?" asked Leo.

"All I had left to pawn was the Rolex I'd planned to give Derek as a wedding present," said Besi, her tone wistful. "Jones used it to buy a gun for the hitman he'd hired. Anyway, like I said, Jones was impatient. I think he was getting worried that I might stab him in the back after Elizabeth was dead, so he decided to blackmail Derek—behind my back."

"How did Jones find out why Derek was fired?" asked Leo.

Besi sighed. "That was my fault. I was cooped up with Jones and I confided in him things I shouldn't have. I told him about Derek's gambling and how he'd embezzled two million dollars from Hennessy Capital. Jones and I did get close. He confided in me about when Elizabeth contacted him and how he found the letter from Guillermo to mama and how he stole my DNA. He filled in all of the blanks for me."

"Did you kill Jones?" asked Leo.

"I didn't want to," said Besi. "But, Jones knew too much … and there really is no such thing as a one-time payment to a blackmailer. It's a lifetime commitment. I had to get rid of everyone who knew the truth, or I would never really have my life back."

"And what about Skip Taylor?" asked Leo.

"All I wanted from Skip was that blue file Jones had given him," said Besi. "I didn't want to kill Skip. When I broke into his rental house, I didn't shoot to kill, even though I could have. I was trying to scare him, so he would get out of the house, and I could look for that file."

"If Jones was blackmailing Derek about his termination," said Leo, "then why did he give Skip the DNA test results that showed you weren't Sam Beaumont's daughter."

"Jones claimed that he'd accidentally put the DNA results in the file he gave to Skip," said Besi. "Why he had a copy of them in the first place, he couldn't say. But, I'm not stupid. Jones kept those DNA results close at hand to hold over my head. To keep me in line. Jones and I worked together against Elizabeth, but eventually, he would have stabbed me in the back. That's why he had to go."

Leo took a deep breath, trying to reconcile the Besi he'd grown up with and the cold-blooded, callous woman standing in front of him. Where was the sweet, caring girl he'd known? Had finding out that Samuel wasn't her father turned her heart to stone? Or, had Besi Beaumont always been, secretly, capable of homicide? Maybe the idea of losing everything she held dear had driven her to commit murder.

"I was keeping tabs on Skip," said Besi. "I knew he liked to walk around the lake behind the hospital in the afternoons. One day, I met him out there, and we had a conversation. He didn't recognize me with the dark hair and sunglasses. I told him I was Jones' girl and I wanted the file."

"You really thought he would give it to you?" asked Leo.

"Didn't hurt to ask," said Besi. "He refused to give it to me. I figured it was somewhere in this house, but I couldn't find it. So, I decided to offer to pay Skip for the file and if he refused, well ..."

"You would kill him?" asked Leo.

"I'd like to know the answer to that ..." said a familiar voice, behind him.

43

Gasping, Vivian spun around, relieved to see the man whose voice she recognized.

"Detective François, thank—"

Vivian's gratitude was cut short by several bullets.

Screaming, she saw, peripherally, a blur of movement. In front of her, the detective charged forward, yelling commands. "Put the gun down and your hands up!"

Unsure of what was happening, or what to do, Vivian turned, and—

Something hard slammed into the back of her head. Crying out, Vivian pitched forward but was yanked back as an arm snaked around her neck. Cold metal pressed against her temple.

"Stay back!" Besi's voice was inches from her ear, loud and panicked. "Stay away, or I will blow her head off!"

Trembling, Vivian froze, staring at Leo, Detective François, and the two deputies flanking the detective, their weapons drawn.

"Besi, let her go," said Leo. "Please."

"Ms. Beaumont, just put the gun down," said Detective François. "This doesn't have to end badly."

"Take me instead," said Leo, taking a step forward. "Let Vivian go, and I will make sure that you get off the island—"

"Shut up and do not come any closer!" screamed Besi, yanking Vivian backward, causing her to stumble.

"Besi, listen to me," said Leo, hands raised as he inched forward. "You'll have a much better chance if you take me."

"He's right, Ms. Beaumont," said Detective François. "Believe it, or not, but if you want to get off this island, I think you should take Mr. Bronson up on his offer."

"How could you say something like that?" Vivian glared at the detective. "Leo can't—"

"Mr. Bronson has significantly more resources than you do, Mrs. Bronson," said François.

"The detective is right," said Leo, staring at her.

Focusing on her husband, Vivian caught an almost imperceptible signal in his blue eyes as his gaze shifted to the left, away from her. Leo was trying to tell her something, she realized. He'd given her a sign with his eyes. What was he trying to tell her?

"You should take my husband," said Vivian. "You know how much money his mom has and you know that Burt has connections, so—"

"Just shut up!" Besi screamed, her hot, dry breath slanting across Vivian's cheek. "I don't want Leo's money or any connections!"

"Then what do you want, Ms. Beaumont?" asked the detective. "Tell me how I can help you?"

"Oh, now you want to help me?" Besi scoffed. "Where was all your help when Elizabeth Davis knocked me over the head and stole my life?"

"Besi, I know what Elizabeth and Aaron Jones did to you was wrong," said Vivian, grunting as Besi tightened her hold and pressed the barrel of the gun harder against Vivian's head. "And you have every right to feel as though Elizabeth and Jones got what they deserved—"

"If you don't shut up with your trite psychobabble," warned Besi, "you're going to get a bullet in the head!"

Vivian flinched, but when she looked at Leo, his gaze seemed to have drifted away from her. Was he looking at something behind her?

"You don't want to do that, Ms. Beaumont," said the detective. "You're already in enough trouble. You don't want to—"

"Don't tell me what I want," Besi cried. "You have no idea what I want!"

"Then, tell me, Ms. Beaumont," said François. "What do you—"

"Derek!" Besi said. "I want Derek. I need him. Where is he?"

"If we get Mr. Hennessy down here," said the detective. "Then you'll let Mrs. Bronson go?"

"I need to talk to Derek," said Besi, her voice hoarse with choked emotion. "I'm not saying another word until you call my fiancé and tell him that I need him! Now!"

"I'll call Mr. Hennessy, but you have to do something for me, as well," said François. "I want you to lower the gun and—"

"I'm not lowering the gun," said Besi. "You tell Derek to come now, or so help me, I will—"

The gunshot was deafening, almost as loud as Besi's high-pitched scream in Vivian's ear. Confused and shocked, Vivian cried out as Besi dropped to her knees.

Detective François and Leo rushed toward her.

Crying, Vivian collapsed against Leo as he grabbed her in a protective embrace and pulled her away from the chaotic scene. Cursing, Besi screamed and kicked at the deputies with her good leg. The other leg was motionless, a pool of blood spreading across the hardwood from beneath her calf.

"It's okay, babe," whispered Leo, kissing her forehead.

"I don't understand," said Vivian, staring up at her husband. "What happened?"

"Officer Fields snuck into the house and positioned himself behind you and Besi," said Leo. "He shot her in the back of the leg."

"Oh, God, Leo." Vivian pressed her cheek against his chest, glaring at Besi Beaumont as Detective François, Officer Fields, and the deputies converged on Besi, wrestling the gun from her, and then arresting her, placing her in handcuffs.

EPILOGUE

"Derek is still sticking by Besi," said Leo as he walked into Vivian's office and dropped down on the couch. "It's been a week since she was arrested, made bail, and was remanded to house arrest and he hasn't left her side."

Turning away from her computer, Vivian leaned back in her creaky chair. "Are you surprised?"

Leo scoffed. "Am I surprised that Derek Hennessy is pulling out all the stops to get his real fiancée cleared of the charges against her? Surprisingly no, I'm not surprised."

Vivian frowned. "You're not?"

Shrugging, Leo said, "After Besi was arrested and that night I had to tell Dad and Derek everything that went down at the Dove Street house in Oyster Farms, there was something about the way Derek looked when he found out everything."

"How did he look?" asked Vivian.

Leo propped his feet on the arm of the couch. "Can't explain it. I thought he'd be pissed and outraged, but he was … I don't know. He was overjoyed to find out that Besi was still alive. He didn't seem to care that she'd killed two people. He was sympathetic and kind. He was upset with himself that he hadn't been able to realize that Elizabeth Davis was fooling him. He was eager to see Besi. He wanted to tell her that he loved her and he wanted to prove to her that he didn't want to marry her for her money."

"Kind of hard to marry Besi for her money when she doesn't have any money," said Vivian.

Leo said, "She's not the Beaumont heiress, but Adrienne Beaumont came from money, and when she died, she left most of her money to Besi."

"So, there's the defense fund," said Vivian.

"I don't think there's enough money in the world to get Besi cleared of double homicide," said Leo. "But, don't tell Derek that. He's convinced that Besi will get off because Elizabeth Davis and Aaron Jones drove her to murder. If they hadn't blackmailed her, she wouldn't have turned homicidal."

"Besi became homicidal when she found out she wasn't the real Beaumont heiress," said Vivian.

"Good luck getting Derek to believe that," said Leo. "He's claiming that the devil made Besi do it."

Vivian sighed. "I think it's hard for everyone to believe that Besi isn't Samuel Beaumont's daughter."

"Everyone except for my mom," said Leo.

"What do you mean?" Vivian asked, leaning forward, putting her elbows on the desk.

"I talked to her this morning," said Leo, sitting up and swinging his legs to the floor. "She and Adrienne grew up in Paris together. Mom says Adrienne was never really a one-man kind of woman. Things only got worse when she married Samuel Beaumont, a man twice her age. Adrienne had a lot of lovers, according to Mom."

"One of which was Besi's father," said Vivian.

Nodding, Leo said, "Mom says there is probably no way to figure out who Besi's dad is. Adrienne was into one-night-stands."

"A hit-it-and-quit-it queen," said Vivian.

"Ironically, Mom said the one guy Adrienne didn't sleep with was Guillermo Davis," said Leo. "Samuel thought they were having an affair, but Adrienne and Guillermo were just good friends. When Adrienne got pregnant with Elizabeth, she thought the baby's father was one of her anonymous hook-ups. She feared Samuel thought the baby was Guillermo's, so she convinced Guillermo to take the child."

"Didn't Samuel wonder what happened to the baby?" asked Vivian.

"Mom said that Adrienne told Samuel the baby was stillborn," said Leo. "A few months later, she and Samuel were having relations again, as my mother put it. But, at the same time, Adrienne was secretly sleeping around."

Vivian shook her head. "So, when she got pregnant a second time, she assumed the baby was Samuel's?"

"Either that," said Leo, "or she didn't want to send another little girl away to live with Guillermo Davis."

Standing, Vivian walked to the couch and sat down on Leo's lap. "Adrienne Beaumont's lies have ruined so many lives. Besi and Elizabeth never got a chance to be sisters. Elizabeth grew up without a mother. Samuel never got to meet his real daughter. Besi has no idea who her father is."

Leo slipped an arm around her waist and kissed her cheek. "Lies do ruin lives. That's why they shouldn't be told. Truth hurts sometimes, but a lie is always worse."

Vivian said, "So, let's promise not to lie to each other, no matter what."

Caressing her cheek, Leo said, "No lies. Veritas omnia vincit."

"Truth conquers all," said Vivian, pressing her mouth against his.

If you enjoyed UNTIL DEATH DO US PART, you'll love the next book in the series – NO ONE WILL FIND YOU!

In the bedroom of a mansion near the sea, a handcuffed man struggles against his restraints.

He can't remember how he was captured, but there's a woman in the room with him. Walking toward him, she smiles as she holds a knife...

He knows he's going to die.

And he knows who's going to kill him.

When the man's body washes up on a pristine white sand beach, married journalists Vivian and Leo Bronson search for answers. After finding out the victim was killed in a ritualistic murder, they uncover an ultra-secret cult whose members perform bizarre rituals.

Going undercover to get the truth, Vivian and Leo find themselves face to face with a demented killer who believes that murder is a sacrifice worth making ...

Get your copy of NO ONE WILL FIND YOU now!

EXCLUSIVE OFFER

Rachel Woods entertains readers with her riveting mysteries, from cozies to whodunits. Now you can get one of her short stories for FREE, when you sign up to join her newsletter:

GET MY FREE SHORT STORY NOW

https://BookHip.com/PTTPAL

ALSO BY RACHEL WOODS

REPORTER ROLAND BEAN COZY MYSTERIES

Roland "Beanie" Bean, husband and loving father, finds himself the unwitting participant in solving crimes as he seeks to make a name for himself as a reporter for the *Palmchat Gazette*.

EASTER EGG HUNT MURDER

MERRY CHRISTMAS MURDER

TRICK OR TREAT MURDER

PALMCHAT ISLANDS MYSTERIES

Married journalists, Vivian and Leo, manage the island newspaper while solving crimes as they chase leads for their next story.

UNTIL DEATH DO US PART

NO ONE WILL FIND YOU

YOU WILL DIE FOR THIS

DON'T MAKE ME HURT YOU

THE PALMCHAT ISLANDS MYSTERIES BOX SET: BOOKS 1 - 4

SPENCER & SIONE SERIES

Gripping romantic suspense series with steamy romance, unpredictable plot twists and devastating consequences of deceit.

HER DEADLY MISTAKE

HER DEADLY DECEPTION

HER DEADLY THREAT

HER DEADLY BETRAYAL

HER DEADLY ENCOUNTER

THE SPENCER & SIONE SERIES BOX SET: BOOKS 1 - 5

MURDER IN PARADISE SERIES

A series of stand-alone romantic mystery novels all set in the fictional Palmchat Islands.

THE UNWORTHY WIFE

THE PERFECT LIAR

THE SILENT ENEMY

ABOUT THE AUTHOR

Rachel Woods studied journalism and graduated from the University of Houston where she published articles in the Daily Cougar. She is a legal assistant by day and a freelance writer and blogger with a penchant for melodrama by night. Many of her stories take place on the islands, which she has visited around the world. Rachel resides in Houston, Texas with her three sock monkeys.

For more information:
www.therachelwoods.com
rachel@therachelwoods.com

facebook.com/therachelwoodsauthor
instagram.com/therachelwoodsauthor
bookbub.com/authors/rachel-woods
amazon.com/author/therachelwoods

ABOUT THE PUBLISHER

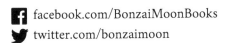

BonzaiMoon Books is a family-run, artisanal publishing company created in the summer of 2014. We publish works of fiction in various genres. Our passion and focus is working with authors who write the books you want to read, and giving those authors the opportunity to have more direct input in the publishing of their work.

For more information:
www.bonzaimoonbooks.com
info@bonzaimoonbooks.com

facebook.com/BonzaiMoonBooks
twitter.com/bonzaimoon

Made in the USA
Middletown, DE
13 June 2023

32486557R00116